The Feared

V. Mull

Author

V. Mull

Young Adult Fantasy Novelist

Published by Underwater Ally Publishing
Copyright © 2022
All Rights Reserved

Visit authorvmull.org for more information.

Cover artist: Jessica Dueck www.jessicadueck.com

For my Grammy, Patricia LaFreniere, and my Nana, Mary Fountain, who always fueled my passion for writing.

Thank you!

To my parents, my aunts, uncles, and cousins, and to my dear friends, for your continued encouragement and support - it's what keeps me going.

To my sister, Beth, for taking time from her chaos-filled days to pull me from the depths of my writer's block. Many of the scenes wouldn't be here today without your help.

To my editor, Donise, who has been dedicated to each of my stories. My books would be filled with goofy mistakes and characters who smile too much without you!

To my A15 moms, for always being there with kind words, advice, and love when I need it.

To my cover artist, Jessica Dueck, for working endlessly with me to perfect the most beautiful cover I've ever seen.

Table of Contents

Chapter 1

Emmeline Foster's dreams were always vivid, realistic, and sometimes frightening. While lifelike dreaming was normal among many people, these dreams were different. They felt beyond the realm of her mind, with the detailed trees and fields of places she'd never been, but especially the people … the person. A man.

Emmeline awoke from a colorful dream on a breezy Sunday morning. She recalled the warm skin of his hand in hers and still felt the familiar fluttering of butterflies in her stomach when he kissed her.

She floated to the bathroom, cursing her alarm clock for taking him away, and ran a brush through her dark, auburn hair. Clothed in a bright yellow floral dress, she pulled on a jean jacket and tried to remember his face. She could only make out the faint frame of his jaw and his crystal eyes, but the color eluded her. It didn't matter because she shivered just thinking about him looking at her.

"The Dad-cab is leaving in one minute," her dad called up the stairs. "Consider this your personal invitation."

"Dad jokes." Jainey, her older sister, stood in the bathroom door and rolled her eyes. Emmeline smirked and set down the brush.

"Did you guys know there are over thirty-eight species on the endangered list?" Emmeline announced as she climbed into the car behind her mother and father.

"Thanks for the random fact." Jainey buckled her seatbelt.

"I just think it's sad. I like animals."

"Okay, Snow White." Making snarky remarks was Jainey's favorite hobby. Though she was two years older than seventeen-year-old Emmeline, they were best friends. Emmeline knew Jainey's teasing was her love language, so she embraced it.

"Here we are. You girls be on your best behavior," their father said.

"Sure thing, Joey boy." Jainey clicked her tongue and winked while snapping a finger at him.

"That's *Dad*, to you, young lady," Maud said, their overly stern mother.

"I'm not standing next to you," Emmeline told her sister as they walked to the door. "You constantly try to make me laugh when the entire church is quiet, and I look like an idiot." She remembered one time Jainey had quietly put her pulled hang-nail on Emmeline's lap while she was distracted by the sermon.

"Who, me? I'd never try to make you look stupid!" Jainey stuck a finger up her nose and brought her front teeth over her bottom lip, making herself look like a rabbit. Emmeline snorted and elbowed her.

- ᘓᘏᐧᕐᘏ -

As mass continued, Emmeline tried to keep her attention on the sermon and *off* Jainey's ridiculous, subtle faces, but her

2

mind wandered to a daydream of strolling through the woods with the man of her dreams.

She was unaware he was sitting only three pews behind her.

"I'm going downstairs to snag a doughnut before Mrs. Bartlet tries to recruit me for the choir again," Jainey said after the priest and altar boys left the large room. She twirled, flipping her chestnut hair, and left the pew. She had a beautiful voice, but suffered from stage fright, though she wouldn't admit it. Emmeline raised an eyebrow at her sister while watching her stride to the double door exit.

A doughnut sounds good, Emmeline thought. She took her purse and coat and ambled from the pew to join the group of parishioners leaving the room. She passed an older gentleman and a younger guy, who were still seated. Emmeline noticed the young man's expression as he leaned forward, gawking at her.

She smiled politely and walked by, her heart beating like a drum, not because she felt awkward for the specific attention, but because she was unusually calmed by his face, which made her uncalm, funny enough. She shook away the feeling and entered the church kitchen where a few people were talking and pouring pots of coffee and tea for one another.

"Hi, Honey," Judy, a sweet woman Emmeline had known since she was young, said when she saw Emmeline. "I cooled some tea for you."

"Thank you," the girl smiled and took the cup.

"Emmeline, is it?" a gravelly voice said from behind.

She turned to see the same man and guy from the pew

3

entering the kitchen. When had he learned her name?

Again, the older man spoke. "I'm George Emsworth." He held his hand out, which Emmeline shook.

"Yes, that's me. Nice to meet you."

George turned to the boy. "This is my grandson, Archibald."

Archie, the name shouted in her mind. She took his hand, and her eyes locked with his. He stared down at her intently with familiar eyes.

Crystal eyes.

"Hi," she whispered.

"You don't remember me, do you?" He blinked, a sort of sadness painted on his otherwise soft expression.

"You look familiar. I'm so bad at remembering names." She laughed nervously.

"I guess it *has* been a while."

"I'll give you two a minute to catch up." The grandfather patted Archibald on the back and hobbled out on his cane.

Everyone had left the kitchen to join together at the long tables to talk, eat doughnuts, and drink coffee, leaving Archibald and Emmeline alone.

"You truly don't remember me?" He took a step closer, towering at least a foot over her.

She swallowed and decided to trust her instincts. "Ar … Archie?"

"Yes." His face relaxed. "That's what you always called me."

"It's on the tip of my tongue where I know you from." She scrunched her brow.

"It took me a few months to remember you, Emmy."

EMMY!

She gasped but certainly couldn't admit that this was the man in every vivid dream she had. His face, she thought, was always a mystery in her sleep, but the freckles sprinkled over the bridge of his nose, and his dimples sparked something in her memory, and absolutely no one called her Emmy except for him in the dreams. She took in the rest of his features - his pepper-blond hair brushed to the side. The jawline she definitely remembered, but the outfit was new. A black leather jacket, blue shirt, and jeans was never how he looked in her mind.

"I *know* you." Emmeline squinted at Archie. How likely was it that someone would meet a dream person … one they'd never known in their whole life?

"You do."

She bit her lip. Making her brain work when put on the spot was not one of her strengths.

Before she could say anything, he pulled a small, wooden figure from his pocket. "I made this for you."

Those words were all it took for memories to flood her mind. Emmeline and another girl, who had expensive garments draped over her arms, walked through the dirt streets filled with yelling merchants selling this and that. There was a rattling, then screaming, then chaotic laughter. Flying through the streets in his small horse-drawn cart was the crazy old man who lived in the hills outside the city. The girl next to Emmeline ran, yelling for her to follow, but Em stood, dumbfounded. As the horse wildly drew closer, someone crashed into her, rolling her out of the streets.

Archie.

He had shown up later that evening, after Emmeline had been tended to by a physician. The servants reluctantly let him in, and he presented her with a small, carved wolf. "I made this for you," he'd said, "to make you feel better."

She was pulled from this odd memory by her sister's demanding voice.

"Yo, Emmeline. We're leaving."

Emmeline bit her tongue like she was trying to keep from snapping at Jainey for the interruption.

"We'd better get going, too." Archibald paused. "Can I have your number?"

Emmeline smiled and grabbed a napkin from the counter, shuffled in her purse for a pen, and scribbled down her home phone number.

Jainey raised her eyebrows and put a hand on her hip. Either she was being overprotective, or she was about to bombard her little sister with a hoard of invasive questions. Either way, Emmeline couldn't wait to continue the conversation with Archie. More so, she wanted to be in absolute silence to tap into her mind of realistic memories. She couldn't decide if they were true or if it was her projecting her dreams.

Unfortunately, being with her family was anything but quiet. Normally, she was grateful for the loving, sometimes annoying, family she was born into. But in the car, she wished more than ever her mom and sister would stop belting the hymns (purposefully bad) from earlier and let her think in peace.

"Wanna tell me who that guy was?" Jainey plopped onto Emmeline's bed after they got home.

"Archie." Emmeline focused on changing into comfy pants and thick, fuzzy socks.

"You guys go to school together?"

"Nope."

"You obviously know each other."

"We just met."

"That's definitely a lie. You two were so lovey dovey it was making me sick."

Emmeline looked her sister in the eye. "I don't care for your jokes. You've no idea what my feelings are for him, nor his for me."

Jainey sat up straight and furrowed her brow.

Her little sister blinked. "Sorry."

"Since when do you speak like Elizabeth Bennet?"

Emmeline looked down and bit the inside of her cheek without answering.

"Whatever." Jainey left the room.

Emmeline rubbed her forehead as she sat at the desk in front of her window, staring at the furry, pink phone. She'd have to grab it the minute it rang or else her parents would answer from the kitchen phone.

Eleven p.m. rolled around, and she awoke to find she'd been in a dead sleep at her desk. It was dreamless, to her surprise. She wiped her eyes and tiptoed to the bathroom to get ready for bed.

As she stared at herself in the mirror, she wondered if her daydreams were becoming a problem. Was it possible that, when everyone left the church kitchen, she imagined a romantic encounter with the dream guy? Was Jainey's inquiry a continuation of her hallucinations?

With tears wetting her eyes, she climbed under the thick comforter and snuggled into a pile of flannel-cased pillows. She prayed to God there would be no dreams for her own sanity.

There were none.

— ⚬⚭⚬⚮⚬⚭⚬ —

"You done PMSing?" Jainey asked her sister when she walked into the kitchen the next morning.

"Jainey," their mother warned.

Emmeline said nothing. The mindless sleep made her lethargic and even sadder. She took a box of cereal and poured it in silence.

Maud handed her daughter the jug of milk from the fridge and looked at her. "Are you okay?"

No. "Yeah." She poured the milk. "Just didn't get the best sleep."

Maud took a sip from her mug. Their mom only let them stay home from school if the thermometer said they had a fever. Lack of sleep never mattered.

"Mom, can I stay home today?" Emmeline decided to challenge the fever rule. "I just need a day, mentally." She stood in anticipation as Maud stirred a spoon around in her sugar-filled coffee.

After a few moments, her mom turned and said, "Okay, but drink water and sit in the sun for at least twenty minutes, even if you have to bundle up. I'll pick up your schoolwork on my way home."

"Thank you." Emmeline was relieved she'd be alone for the day.

She threw her head back and sighed when her parents and sister left for work half an hour later. She locked the door and sat on the couch, covering herself in a knitted blanket, and eyed the telephone hanging on the wall.

Emmeline decided to get a bowl of chips and turn on the local news. She was invested in a story about a woman who had escaped a max-security prison a few months back, so the ringing sound didn't register as important right away. When it did, she nearly knocked the bowl off the couch.

"Hello?"

"Yes, hello, I'm looking for Mister Joseph Foster."

"I'm sorry, he's not home at the moment. May I take a message?" Emmeline wrote down that her dad needed to call some guy named Geoffrey. She went back to her snack and blanket.

The phone didn't startle her the second time it rang.

"Hello?"

"Emmy?"

Now she was startled. She held the phone away from her face as she took a deep breath. "Archie?"

"Yes, hi," he sighed in relief. It seemed he thought she'd forgotten him again.

"I was beginning to imagine ..."

"It wasn't real? I was afraid of that."

"What did you mean when you said it took months to remember me?"

"Grandfather told me something, and I thought he was delusional until I began remembering the past. It started out as dreams, then blinding flashes in my mind as I went about the day. Finally, it was the truth that invaded my mind."

"What was the truth?" She stretched the phone cord to the couch where she could sit, wrapped in the blanket.

"Will you speak with me in person?"

"My parents would grind me to dust if you came over without them here to supervise."

"Grandfather will be with me." His voice was deep, smooth, and soothing.

"Okay."

Another moment of silence. "Where do you live?" he chuckled.

"Twenty-eight Willow Lane in Monmouth."

"I'll see you in fifteen minutes." Archie hung up.

Emmeline ran to the bathroom to put on eyeliner and make sure her hair didn't look like a complete rat's nest. She let loose the ponytail, twirled her hair, and was done. She smiled at herself. Almost no makeup, no effort on her hair. It was weird … if she left the house, she wanted to make sure her hair wasn't gross, and her face wasn't blank. But her face looked *right* this time.

The knock at the door made her jump. She approached it, inhaled, exhaled, and turned the knob.

Mr. Emsworth was standing there with a big smile, wearing his brown suit and perfectly sanded cane. Archie stood behind looking nervous.

Emmeline moved to the side to welcome them in and

offered them a drink.

"I'd love an ice water, dear," George said, happily inspecting the family photos on the kitchen wall.

Archie said nothing while Emmeline dropped ice cubes into a glass and turned on the faucet. Once the man gulped the water down, he said, "Lovely. Would you show me to the restroom?" He continued to grin while hobbling on his cane after her.

As the bathroom door clicked closed, Archie stood at the end of the hall and held out his hand. Emmeline walked to him and took it.

The dream. His warmth was familiar.

"So," she began.

"So." They sat on the couch.

"You were saying on the phone … what truth did you remember?"

Archie let go of her hand and sat up. "Our life together."

Chapter 2

Emmeline stood. "Our *what*?"

"I get it, Emmy. It was a bombshell for me, too. I know it'll take time to remember ... *if* you remember." He looked away.

She could see him hiding the tears in his eyes. The urge to stop his pain was overwhelming. She sat back down.

"I've had dreams," she began. Archie turned. "I could never see his full face, but I think you *are* him."

The sweet side smile he gave was her answer. It wasn't a hoax, it wasn't her overactive imagination, and it wasn't a lie. The person sitting beside her was real flesh and bone. *Real*.

"I still don't get it," she admitted.

"I don't blame you. Reincarnation is a tough pill to swallow."

That word wasn't what she was expecting. In truth, she wasn't expecting anything, but that was completely off the wall.

"Reincar-*WHAT?*" Things blew through her mind while she stood again and paced the living room.

"How do you explain the dreams?" he interrupted her thoughts. "How do you explain the memories? I know you felt them yesterday."

"Dreams are always weird and never make sense," she

tried to counter.

"But you remembered what you called me."

"Archie is a normal nickname for anyone named Archibald." Emmeline knew she was making excuses, but she continued to defend logic.

"You risked your life for me." He left the couch to be near her.

Emmeline gaped at him.

"The fever that took my parents ... I got it, and I wanted you to leave. I begged you to go, but you wouldn't. You stayed there night and day. I don't even know if you slept, but every time I was conscious, there you were with that beautiful smile and a funny joke to lighten the mood."

Imagination couldn't paint the image in her mind. It was a real, raw memory. Watching him sob while they attended his parents' funeral, seeing his face pale and the energy leave his body as his muscles gave out ... she remembered.

It was the year 928, a week after his parents died, when Emmeline caught Archie and held his arm over her shoulder. He'd been crying, telling her every happy memory he had of his parents. She supported his weight as they walked back to his manor. Grandfather ran out of the door when he saw them coming and carried Archie the rest of the way.

"I'm staying," Emmeline insisted. Grandfather's grateful and kind smile was so clear in her mind that when she looked over her shoulder to see Grandfather standing in the hallway back in the present day, it was as if no time had passed.

"It's true," she stated.

"Welcome back, my dear." Grandfather George used his cane to walk into the living room and hug Emmeline. She embraced him, remembering he had been like a grandfather to her as well.

Tears rolled down Archie's face. "So, you believe us?"

She nodded, tears now spilling down her own cheeks. She ran to him and threw her arms around his waist, letting him envelop her completely.

Archie squeezed her closer. "Emmy, we found each other."

Chapter 3

"You were married in the year 930, do you remember?" George asked while the three sat around the table.

"The memories are still unclear," she admitted.

"That's okay." Archie put his hand over hers. "Your dress was beautiful." He looked out the window like he was seeing her through it.

Emmeline's smile faded as she recognized the sorrow in his eyes.

"It was right after our wedding …" Fear crept into her mind. Now, flashes of their coach zigzagging down the dirt path through the Hemlock Woods invaded her brain - her head hitting the gold-trimmed interior as the wheels bumped over sharp rocks. The driver had been attacked and the horses went crazy with terror. Emmy was screaming while Archie tried to climb from the door to the driver's bench above.

"We'll have to jump," he shouted over the noise. He took her hand and pulled her close. "That patch of moss." He pointed, waiting for the right moment to spring from the coach.

They leaped and rolled. Archie sprained his wrist, and Emmeline's shoulder took the first blow to the ground. She was crying. He crawled to her and pulled her onto his lap.

The newlyweds didn't see who attacked them until they

heard the crunching of leaves and sticks circling them within the dark trees. Creatures in black cloaks stepped from the shadows into the mossy grove.

Emmeline snapped from her memory and cried out. "What happened to us, Archie?"

"We assumed you were the victims of burglary," George said. "Your bodies were never recovered. The king's deputy concluded that you were taken away by a group of bandits to hold you for ransom, but no demands ever reached us."

"The king's deputy took our case?" Emmeline widened her eyes.

"We were of noble blood, dear." George allowed a subtle smile to part his lips partnered with a twinkle in his eye.

"I suppose that explains the extravagant carriage, and the watchmen, and the manor house," she said, then bit her lip. "Can anyone explain this whole second life thing? We were born in the nine-hundreds. Why wouldn't we have been reborn immediately after we died? Where did we go for centuries?"

"You have many questions, Emmeline. Ones I cannot answer."

"This is bizarre." Emmy scratched her head.

"It is. But we're together now. That's the only thing that matters, right?" Archie took her hand.

- ᛟᛉᚱᛟᛁᛟᛉᛟᛟ -

Emmeline laid in bed that evening with a notebook, writing

down every single memory; the things she dreamed, the things she'd learned in the past two days, and the things she believed to be true. She kept glancing at the phone, mad at herself for not getting her husband's – *boyfriend's?* – number. She had been too preoccupied with begging them to take her along.

It rang.

She leapt for it, knocking a pen jar off the desk.

"Hello?" she nearly yelled.

"Love," Archie replied, again with a relieved sigh.

"Archie, I can't stand you being away." Emmeline plopped in her chair and buried her face in her hand.

"We'll figure out a way to properly be together. For now, we must act as children do."

"*Teens*," she corrected.

"Right."

"It's weird. Back then, we were adults. Now we're considered children."

"The world has changed."

"I wish it hadn't. This afternoon my mom grilled me about my homework and plans for college. I wanted to just scream that I was going to live with my husband."

Silence followed for a few seconds until he said, "I've prayed every day for us to continue our life together ever since I saw the truth. We're blessed, Emmy. We have a chance to live a long life now."

Emmeline knew what he meant. The probability of death during childbirth was low. There were vaccines to protect from fatal diseases. Fevers were simply inconvenient, not a threat to life.

But it felt wrong. This world, her family. Since her memories began to come to her, she felt out of place, like she was living a lie.

"No. No, Archie. I want to go home," she spoke quietly into the receiver.

"We don't even know how we got here."

"So, we don't stop until we find a way back."

"What about your family?"

Here in twentieth-century America, she had two parents and a sister. When she was born the first time, her mother passed away in childbirth, and her father died after an arrow pierced his heart while leading his men in the battle of Brunanburh when she was fourteen. Emmeline then lived as the ward of Lord Allistair Caliburn, her father's brother. And while this family felt offbeat, they'd still raised her, and she loved them dearly.

"What if there's a way to bring them with us?"

"Em, I'm not sure if that's …"

"You can't seriously want to give up and just stay here like this. We were married. I love my family, but them treating me like a child when I've already lived as a full-grown adult is starting to burn my bacon."

"Burnt bacon is the worst."

"Archie," Emmeline warned.

He sighed. "I made this for you."

That sentence was more meaningful than centuries of "I love yous," and her cry came out as a single laugh.

"Can you actually give it to me next time?" She wiped her eyes.

"Only if you promise not to lose it."

"I wouldn't lose it!"

"Emmy, you lose everything."

"Oh, eat my shorts, Archibald."

His laugh burst through the receiver. "Today's speech is much different than where we came from."

"Yeah." She closed her eyes, imagining his freckles and soft hair. As she was about to ask him to meet her somewhere, her mom knocked on the door.

"Time to hang up," she said.

Emmeline wanted to scream. How dare anyone tell her to stop talking to her own husband.

"I'll call you tomorrow. I love you beyond a lifetime, Emmy." Archie clicked the phone.

Emmeline ground her teeth. She took a deep breath to calm herself.

"Who was that?" Maud asked.

Emmy decided to go with a half-truth that would satisfy her mom. "His name is Archie. I've been talking to him for a while, and we decided to date."

Her mom looked like a foghorn was just blown into her face.

"He's really nice, Mom. You might have even seen him. He goes to our church."

"Why don't you invite him for lunch next Sunday?"

"Sure." Emmeline was nervous about the thought. Her parents would never let her go out with anyone, even friends, without meeting them first. It was their way of protecting her, and she generally didn't mind, but this was so different, now that she had her memories, and now that it was Archie. "I planned on meeting him tomorrow after school."

"Not on a school night."

Emmy would need a stress ball to squeeze every time she was bossed around from now on. "My homework will get done, and I won't stay up late. It'll only be for a few hours. His grandfather invited me for dinner."

Her mother thought for a moment. "How about I drop you off and meet them both?"

"Okay. And he can drive me home."

"I don't know about that."

"Ask his grandfather for his driving record," Emmeline snapped.

"Emmeline, what is with you?"

Her face burned. She had better be careful, or she'd be prevented from seeing Archie altogether. "Sorry. My brain is just mush today."

"I'll let you get some sleep. No more phone calls tonight, okay?"

Emmy nodded, wishing she had her own phone line, but heard Archie's voice in her head. "Patience, sweetheart."

Chapter 4

"This is George Emsworth, and this is Archie." Emmeline turned to the men. "This is Maud, my mother," she said after she and her mom arrived at Grandfather's house. That morning, before Emmeline left for school, Archie called her, and she finally remembered to get his number. Then she informed him about the plan for after school.

George welcomed Maud and Emmeline inside after they shook hands.

"Now when did you join our church?" Maud added sugar and sipped the coffee Grandfather poured for her.

"About four or five weeks ago." He sat on the couch next to his grandson.

"You must have been going to different mass times, then."

"Most likely. We usually go to the early morning mass. It was only this past Sunday we chose to sleep in a bit."

"Oh, I thought you said you two met a few weeks ago," she said to her daughter.

"Archibald sometimes goes to the late morning mass without me," Grandfather caught himself.

Emmeline and Archie eyed each other with sly smiles.

⸻ ⚬✶⚬ ⸻

Maud stayed for another ten minutes chatting.

"She seems to be more protective. You're technically my first boyfriend," Emmeline said after her mother left.

"I'm happy you came over today," Archie said, moving across the room and taking a seat next to her, so close that the cushion sank in, sliding her closer to him. The thrill of his arm touching hers fogged her brain and she nearly missed the urgency in his eyes.

"We received something odd in the middle of the night."

"What?"

Grandfather pulled a note from his pocket and handed it over.

Emmy read aloud, "'*You may have found each other, but he will not live.*' What the heck does this mean?"

"It means someone knows we're from the past." Archie leaned forward. "And that we're together again."

"Great, as if we didn't have enough of a challenge trying to travel back in time. Now we gotta dodge creeps." Emmy slouched back and crossed her arms.

"There's more," Grandfather said, getting their attention. "I left out a piece of information about your disappearance. Turn that paper over."

She did and saw a sketch of a star within a crescent moon and a lightning bolt piercing them.

"Those began appearing. First, they showed up in the Hemlock woods sparsely. After that, they were etched into doorways, branded on livestock, drawn in the dirt ... they even made a large one using hay to outline this symbol."

"Did anyone discover what it means?"

"No one saw a fleck of the ones doing it. Guards were placed across towns and villages as each symbol showed up. It was as if ghosts were wreaking havoc, but no one else was robbed or taken by the Feared, as they came to be known."

"So, this is a sort of cult that has lasted for centuries?" Archie asked.

"No, my boy. I believe the Feared have followed us into this lifetime."

"What do they want with us?" Emmeline shrieked.

George thought for a moment. "I truthfully don't know."

Archie turned white as paper. "Our souls."

Chapter 5

"I have to get you home, Emmy." Archie looked at the clock.

Emmeline focused on the moon, star, and bolt symbol, then raised her head. "I think the repercussions of breaking curfew are miniscule compared to having our souls attacked."

"I don't want your mother disliking me already," Archie said.

She sighed. "Fine."

~ ⁂ ~

Archie and Emmeline drove in silence for a few minutes.

"I know this is hard," he said. "I told you how long it took me to come to terms with my current age and needing to follow today's rules."

"But you live with your grandfather, who already knows the truth and treats you the same. My parents have no idea. I had to convince my mom to let me see you."

"You feel you should be able to see me whenever you like?"

"Of course, I do. We should be living together, making a life for ourselves, *back home*."

Archie eyeballed her, then aimed his attention to the

dark road. "I understand your anger. Let me win over your parents by following their rules for just a little while, then I'm sure things will get easier."

"And if the Feared come for us before then?"

"I'm just trying to navigate this life on a day-to-day basis." Archie huffed and fell silent.

"I'm sorry, Arch." Emmy relaxed her arms and took his free hand, which he brought to his lips and kissed. He walked her to the door once they arrived.

She stared into his eyes, so brilliant and bright that even the dim porch light ringed with moths couldn't diminish their gleam. "You want to win over my parents? Come meet my dad." She winked.

- ·◦◦≫·◦≪◦· -

"So, this is Church Boy." Jainey entered the kitchen as Archie, Emmeline, and her parents were talking. "Pleasure to see you again," she said in a badly imitated British accent.

Emmy rolled her eyes and introduced her sister to Archie.

Jainey plopped in a chair across from him and squinted.

"Can you not?" Emmeline chided, but Archie's coy smile showed his amusement.

Her older sister shrugged. "I have to be intimidating."

"That's enough," their dad cut them off. He turned back to the boy. "Where do you go to school?"

"I've graduated, sir."

Maud sat up uncomfortably. "When? How old are

you?"

"Er, eighteen. I graduated last year."

"Do you have plans to go to college?" Joe continued.

"Yes. I took a year off for an internship, but I have since applied to a few state colleges." Archie eyed Emmeline quickly with a slight grin.

"That's very good, very good." Her dad nodded. "What's the plan?"

Emmy was interested to know, too. In the 900s, he was a nobleman and landowner. His goal was to acquire hundreds of acres and hire farmers, loggers, servants, and more. Emmeline always knew he was truly noble for wanting to give people a good living.

She was snapped back to the kitchen with her family when Archie said, "I'll be majoring in Farm and Ranch management."

Emmeline snorted out a laugh which had the whole table looking at her – Archie being the only one grinning from ear to ear, knowing she remembered.

"Now that's one I've never heard of," her dad continued.

"Yes, it's not common."

Emmeline covered her face, pretending she was rubbing her forehead to hide her snickering.

"I'd like to own a couple hundred acres."

"What would you do with a couple hundred acres?" Maud chimed in.

"I want to hire loggers and farmers."

"Maybe some servants?" Emmeline was teary-eyed.

"They're called chefs and house cleaners now." Archie

winked at her.

Confusion was pasted on the faces of everyone else.

"Well, I better get going." Archie pushed his chair out and stood. "It was wonderful meeting you all."

He and Joe shook hands at the door. "You drive safe, young man."

"I'm just going to say bye to him." Emmeline passed her dad and stepped outside.

"Five minutes," her mom called. "It's nearly bedtime."

Joe closed the door.

"Bedtime?" Archie joked.

"Kiss my grits," she raised her brow and giggled. "I had to hold my breath because I was about to burst. Did you see their faces!" She started laughing again.

"If they only knew how good a businessman I truly am," he chortled.

"Oh boy." She wiped her tears.

"I've been thinking about buying land in Scotland."

"*After* we get home … right?" She watched him swallow.

"Yeah, of course." He pulled her into a tight, warm hug.

"Love you, Arch."

Over the next days, Emmeline and Archibald met after she got out of school. She'd eat dinner with him and Grandfather and discuss the information they dug up on the tenth century, trying to find out if anyone in history had written about the Feared.

"Black, winged creatures." Grandfather read, describing fable-like beings. "Wicked and evil."

"That book is labeled fiction and mythological creatures. We're not dealing with fairies, Grandfather," Emmeline said.

"Are we not, my girl?"

"You can't be serious." She raised a brow at him.

"Hold on, Em." Archie put his hand on hers. "You really believe these things exist?" he asked with all seriousness.

Grandfather George used his cane to adjust his bad leg. "I do."

There was a knock at the door. It startled them all so that they sat for a moment, just staring. Archie was the first to stand and moved slowly to the door. Another knock, a pounding, really, made him jump. He twisted the knob and opened it a crack to see a dead bird on the doorstep – beheaded.

"Jesus," he gulped.

"What is it, son?" Grandfather asked.

Archie looked back, fear blazing in his eyes. "A warning."

Chapter 6

Grandfather and Emmeline ran to see the freshly killed animal staining the steps with blood.

"Close the door." Emmeline pulled Archie back and bolted the top lock. "They're out there right now, surrounding us again. I can't go home."

Archie looked at his grandfather. "She's right," he said.

"Now hold on, kids." Grandfather put his hand in the air. "I've seen this scare tactic many times. They haven't prepared their final attack. This is only to frighten you, otherwise they wouldn't bother."

"She should at least stay a little bit longer," Archie argued.

"Right." Grandfather nodded. "Give your parents a call, Emmeline, and I'll make us some hot tea." Grandfather limped to the kitchen.

After hanging up with her mom, Emmeline sucked her teeth. "Well, she's pissed."

"I think your safety comes before them liking me at this point."

"Agreed." Em glanced at George coming back to the living room with a kettle and three mugs. For the first time, his limp raised some questions. She recalled him being in perfect health in their old lives. "Grandfather, what happened to your leg?"

He looked down and tilted his head. "It's odd ... I don't remember. The last I knew I was visiting with Lord Allistair, walking the grounds, and next I was here with this cane."

"Another reason to get home." She swallowed.

Grandfather wrinkled his brow, so Archie filled him in.

"I never considered it, especially with all this being thrown at us in such a short period of time." George blew into the hot mug. "Is it what you really want?"

Archie looked at Emmeline and held her hand. "She's my wife, and I'll follow her anywhere." He turned back to his grandfather. "If she wants to go back, I do too."

Em smiled gratefully at him.

"Very well then. We'll start our research on how to travel back in time ... however one would start."

- ⚬☜⚬☞⚬ -

Archie surveyed the yard and surrounding trees after opening the door two hours later. "I think it's clear. Come on." He took Emmeline's hand, but she hesitated.

"Ya know, we should have our own name. They call themselves the Feared. We need something cool like that."

"The Fearless," Archie said with a grin.

"I like it." She bobbed her head, lifting her cheeks in a humorous smile.

- ⚬☜⚬☞⚬ -

Archie pulled his car into Emmeline's driveway. He got out

and, again, inspected the trees, listening for sound louder than a chipmunk scurrying through the leaves. No noise came but the crickets playing a nighttime lullaby.

"Good evening, young man," Joe greeted them as they stepped through the door.

"Evening, sir." Archie took the dad's hand.

"It's getting late." Emmeline's mother appeared from the kitchen, wiping her hands on a dishtowel. She held a stern look, nearly glaring at the boy.

Emmeline sighed at her mom's coldness, but Archie grinned, leaned down, and hugged her close, as if sending her messages of "It'll be okay," and "We'll keep each other safe," and "I love you, Emmy."

After the door closed behind her husband, Emmeline went directly to her room. Jainey stood cross-armed in the doorway a moment later.

"Yes?" Emmeline raised her brow.

"It's been how long, and you *still* haven't told me anything about this guy."

"I didn't think you'd be interested."

"Since when?"

Emmeline shrugged.

"Don't I always stick my nose into your business? You never minded before."

"Maybe I mind now," she snapped at Jainey.

Jainey closed the door quietly and turned to her sister who was staring at her from the bed.

"Tell me what's going on. I know something is happening, and I'm not leaving this chair until I find out what." She plopped into Emmeline's swivel chair and crossed her legs.

Emmy snorted. "You'd never believe me if I told you."

"Cliché thing to say, and yet, the other person *always* believes. So, try me."

Emmeline sucked in her lips as she came to a decision. Telling her sister, her best friend, every detail was more of an urge than a choice. So she began from the *very* beginning.

Chapter 7

Jainey gawked at her sister once Emmeline had finished her saga.

"Well?"

Jainey leaned forward. "Remember that time you couldn't taste food for a week, and you thought it was some rare disease, but really you were using expired mouthwash?"

"Uh …"

"Or when you thought you needed to go to the hospital because your skin was turning blue, but it was the new sheets you didn't wash before putting them on your bed? Yeah, this sounds dumber than that. Like, beyond dumber."

Emmeline sighed. "I knew you wouldn't believe me."

Jainey finally rose from the chair and walked to the door. "You should write a book, kid."

Emmeline immediately went to the phone to let Archie know she'd told someone.

"I'm sure she's just shocked," he said.

"Nope. She made some jokes and ditched."

"Maybe it's an immediate reaction for her. She needs time to process the information, just like we had to."

"Maybe."

"I'll see you tomorrow, okay?"

"I heard Mom make a comment to Dad on my way upstairs. She told him she's putting her foot down, and that this obsession with you is unhealthy. I'm going to let her cool off for a day, but call me, okay?"

"Probably for the best. We'll see each other Sunday. She can't stop me from going to church ... I think."

Emmeline laughed.

She crawled into bed after double-checking all the doors and windows were locked in the house. Still, she couldn't sleep that night, nor the next.

- ◦°✧◦┊◦✧°◦ -

Emmeline pulled a sweater over her head on Sunday morning, hoping her mom would have no objection to her going home with Archie after church. She braided her hair, then strolled lazily down the stairs. Upon seeing her enter the kitchen, Jainey commented on Emmeline's outfit, comparing it to a Dr. Seuss truffula tree. The girl shook her head at Jainey, wondering if her jokes meant she was still processing what Emmeline said the other night, or if she was back to her normal self.

George welcomed the Fosters to join him once they arrived at the church. To Emmeline's surprise, Jainey did nothing to try making her sister bust a gut during the sermon.

After Mass, Mrs. Bartlet approached Jainey. She welcomed the conversation, though her face was perplexed, but they were too far away for Emmy to listen in. A moment later, her older sister and the choir director walked out of the room together.

Weird.

"Who is this fine-looking gentleman?" a soft voice asked.

"Hi Judy." Emmeline introduced her to Archie and George.

"Judy," Joe greeted the woman with a nod.

"Morning," she smiled politely. Emmeline had always noticed a certain coldness between her father and Judy, though she didn't know why. The woman was like a second (nicer) mother to Emmeline.

"We'll be headed to the car in about ten minutes," Joe said to his daughter. He nodded, again, to Judy and Archie, then left.

"Well then. It was nice to meet you, Archibald. See you later, Sweetie."

"I don't think your dad likes me too much," Archie said once they were alone.

Emmeline *did* notice her dad getting almost as annoyed as her mom with her constantly being out with Archie and his grandfather. She was hardly ever home anymore.

"Maybe I should stay home today," she told him, feeling guilty she'd caused a ruckus in her family, whom she'd always gotten along with.

Archie looked away and squinted. "Do you still want to go back?"

"Home, yes."

"We need to begin working on that before …"

"The Feared snatch us up like a bag of potatoes."

"I appreciate how you can lighten the doom of a

situation," he chortled. "Come on." His warm hand took hers, and they left together.

- ᓚᘏ♥ᕇᕘᘏᓭ -

The number of messages from Maud recorded on George's answering machine when they arrived back was enough to make all three of them wince.

"We gotta figure this time travel thing out *fast*. My parents might kill me before those fae do."

"Grab your coats, kids. We'll head to the library."

Chapter 8

Attempting to appease her still-angry parents for not asking their permission to go with Archie yesterday, Emmeline came right home after school. She tried calling him after throwing her backpack on the bed and kicking off her shoes, but it went to the answering machine. The phone rang a moment later. It was that guy, Geoffrey.

She, again, tried calling Archie, but he still didn't pick up. Hours went by, and she was getting frustrated and nervous.

"What the hell is going on?" she whispered to herself as the line trilled and went to the answering machine for the umpteenth time. She put the phone on its hook a little too forcefully and left the room. She bit down on her lip while standing outside Jainey's closed door and knocked.

"What?" her sister said. Emmy opened the door.

"I just need someone to talk to."

Jainey spun in her chair, then dramatically offered a hand to welcome her sister into the room.

"I haven't heard from Archie in hours."

"So? He's probably busy."

"Please don't pretend we didn't have that conversation. We're trying to figure out who's targeting us. This is serious."

Jainey looked at the floor.

"Can I at least borrow your car? Please?"

Jainey waved a hand, her way of giving permission, so Emmeline flew down the stairs. She needed to see Archie – to make sure he was okay. Intrusive thoughts filled her mind as she drove her sister's beat-up sedan over pothole-ridden roads. Images of ten-foot demons feasting on her husband's body. She shivered, trying to keep her lunch from coming up.

- ⚭⚭⚭ -

She pulled into the driveway outside the Emsworths' house. Not one light was on. Emmeline pounded on the door, but when no one answered, she sat on the front steps and held in a panicked sob.

Something horrible had happened – she was sure of it. Archie wouldn't leave her waiting this long for anything. He would have told her if he was going to be away.

After ten minutes of crying and shivering in the cold, Archie and Grandfather's car appeared. Emmeline ran to them when they stepped out.

"Where *were* you two? I've been calling all day! I'm ready to beat you with a wet sock for worrying me."

"Sorry, do we know you?" Archie glanced at George.

Emmeline drew back, narrowing her eyes at him. "That's not funny, Archibald."

"Do you need help, dear?" Grandfather set the paper bag of groceries in his hands on the hood of the car.

"What?" she breathed. "It's Emmeline ..."

Archie shook his head and cleared his throat. "It's

38

getting late, and we have to cook dinner. If there's nothing you need, we need to get inside. You should probably get home. I'm sorry," he said again in a pity-filled sympathetic tone.

Emmeline felt lightheaded. It had to be some kind of practical joke. But he'd never been one to trick her, at least not in this malicious way. And Grandfather? He wouldn't condone it.

Archie turned away, looking into the woods. She followed his gaze to a swarm of bees buzzing toward them. Archie began flailing and screaming as they surrounded him. George swatted his cane at them.

"Stop, stop!" Emmeline hollered. She reached through the whirling yellow insects and grabbed Archie's arm. "Don't move and they won't hurt you," she tried to reason.

He wasn't listening. She jumped in and held him as still as her muscles would let her. He blinked, looking down at her. A sort of shine came to his eyes, like a dull haze was wiped away. The bees flew off.

"My God." He ducked his head into her neck and pulled her in close, trying to catch his breath. Grandfather wrapped his arms around them both. "Inside! Quickly now."

"I didn't remember you … I didn't," Archie repeated, gulping.

"Shh," she said. "It's okay." Emmeline rubbed his back.

"Why were there bees? At night? And why didn't they

attack you?"

Emmeline shrugged. "They never have. Fuzzy buzzies like me."

"Ff … fuzzy buzzies?" Archie's mood lightened as Emmy stuck her tongue out at him.

"Wait," she said, her eyes darting around. "Uncle Allistair loved bees. I remember him insisting that he tend to his beehives instead of the farm hands. He taught me how to care for them, too. I was about five when I gave them the name fuzzy buzzies. They never stung Uncle Allistair, either." She smiled and sighed. "Maybe his bees are protecting us." She said it jokingly, but in her mind, she wondered if it could be true.

Archie and Emmeline turned their attention to George, who hadn't said anything, seemingly deep in thought. "We left early this morning to go to the grocery store. It doesn't make sense, it's already so late," George said. The other two remained silent. "Archibald, do you remember anything odd while we were there?"

"No, we went in, shopped, and left. How is it possible that an entire day passed?"

"How is it possible we traveled hundreds and hundreds of years into the future? How is it possible that a group of magical beings are hunting you?" Grandfather asked.

"Wait," Archie looked at the table, remembering something. "We saw your friend from church. Judy."

"Is there something significant about that? It's not unusual she'd be there," Emmy said.

"Yes, it is significant." George tapped the table. "She had no groceries, no cart."

"So?"

"She approached us and struck up a conversation, but it was an odd way to talk."

"You're right," Archie chimed in. "She seemed almost otherworldly. And she asked a lot of questions."

"Are you suggesting Judy, the nicest woman on Earth, had something to do with this," Emmeline waved her hand around, "this … whatever it is?"

"Abduction, or mind tapping, or something."

Emmy threw her head back in frustration at Archie.

"At this point, anything is possible, my dear." George patted her hand.

"I've known her basically my whole life. Well, this life. There's no way."

"She's been watching you," George interrupted her, and she stiffened. "What better way to ensure you never find Archibald than keeping an eye on you."

"You don't want to believe it, I know," Archie said.

"I sure don't," she grumbled. "But … was that *it*? You only talked to her?"

"Yes."

The phone rang, startling them all.

"Hello?" Grandfather answered it. "Yes, I will. Have a good evening." He hung up and turned to the couple. "Your mother wants you home, my dear."

"Perfect."

"Drive straight home and don't talk to anyone, okay?" Archie stood and hugged her. "Also, thanks for saving my life, finally. You owed me." He kissed her head.

"*So* funny." She pressed her lips to his. She then leaned

41

up and kissed George's cheek. "Bye, Grandfather."
Emmeline drove home with her high beams on, scanning
the woods for people. How would she ever sleep again?
She jumped from the car, slammed the door, and sped into
the house so fast she barely noticed her parents and the
stranger sitting at the table, coffee in their hands and shock
on their faces.

"Was an axe murderer chasing you?" Jainey asked
sarcastically, grabbing a water bottle from the fridge. She
smirked and left the room. *Something like that*, Emmy
thought with a gulp, staring at the stranger.

"This is Geoffrey, your father's friend from the bank,"
Maud said, trying to sound happy to see her daughter.
Emmy could see the sternness in her gaze, telling her she
wasn't too thrilled with her daughter, but Emmeline knew
that stone-cold look.

Geoffrey works with Dad?

"Pleased to meet you in person." He stood to greet
Emmeline. "I believe we spoke on the phone a few times."

She reluctantly shook his hand, trying to give him a
polite smile. *Touch my family, and I'll send the bees after you,*
she thought. He tilted his head and Emmy wondered if he
could read her thoughts.

"I'd better head out – don't want to overstay my
welcome. Thanks for the coffee."

"See you tomorrow," Joe said.

Geoffrey nodded, gave Emmy another questionable
glance, and departed. She stared at her parents, worried
their memories had been wiped. She approached the table.

"Is something wrong, Emmeline?" her dad asked. She

blew out a slight breath of relief when her father said her name. She shook her head and bid them goodnight. Though the Feared could probably get through locked doors and windows, she secured them anyway and closed the curtains. Emmeline waited for the sound of her parents' footsteps, and the sound of their bedroom door closing before she picked up the phone at her desk and dialed Archie's number.

"He calls all the time," she said after telling him about finding the stranger in her kitchen. "Which is weird because he supposedly works at the bank with Dad."

"Maybe he works a different shift, or in another area?"

"My dad *does* work in an office on the second floor pretty much all day." Em groaned. "This sucks."

"We have no reason to tell your parents to stay away from him, do we?"

"Uhn-uh." Emmy tapped her blue paint-chipped nails on the desk.

"What about Jainey? You can tell her you think he's dangerous."

"Yeah right, like she believed me before?"

"Emmy, we gotta try."

She finally agreed but told him she'd wait until tomorrow when her sister got home from work. *From the bank with her dad … Oh my God!* "Arch, Jainey works with him, too! They're at the same bank. How am I so stupid I didn't realize?"

"You need to tell her tonight, Em." They hung up and, though she tried to sneak to her sister's room, the panicked shuffle of her slippers made scuffing noises down the carpeted hall. She didn't bother knocking.

"Jesus, Emmeline!" Jainey had multiple books and papers – sheet music, laid across her bed when her little sister burst through the door.

"You can't go to work tomorrow."

"And why not?"

"Geoffrey's evil."

"Come *on*." Jainey let out an exasperated breath.

"No, you gotta listen to me." She grabbed her sister's arms.

"And what exactly would I tell Dad?"

"Fake sick or something. Come with me to Archie's tomorrow. I'll skip school."

It was tongue in cheek, Emmy knew. "Fine."

"Really?"

"I'd like to hear what your boyfriend has to say about all this."

Emmeline threw her hands around her sister's neck. "Thank you!"

"Yeah, yeah, now go to bed, fool."

Chapter 9

Morning came, and Jainey had successfully gotten the day off. Emmeline packed her bag and put it on like she was going to school as their parents said goodbye and left for work.

"I assume I have to pretend to be Mom and call you out?"

"Damn skippy."

Jainey gave her the side-eye as she put the phone to her ear.

"Thanks," Emmeline said after Jainey had hung up. "Really."

Her older sister nodded, then grabbed her keys from the hook, opened the door, and drove to the Emsworth's.

Jainey seemed to clench her teeth as Emmy knocked on the door.

"You don't need to knock, Em," Archie said.

"Habit," she replied.

"So, let's get to it." Jainey wasn't one to beat around the bush. Grandfather welcomed them all to sit and began the story.

"It took time for all of us, dear," Grandfather George said while Jainey processed the reiteration of Emmy's story from his point of view. Emmeline was at the edge of her seat, studying her sister's face. If she wished anyone would believe her, it was Jainey.

The girl licked her lips. "You were all born over a thousand years ago in Scotland, reborn in America, here in the twentieth century, and a bunch of evil faeries are after you?"

"Yes." Archie inhaled and looked at Emmeline, who was struggling to read her sister's bland expression.

"Please believe us," she pleaded.

Jainey intertwined her fingers, still saying nothing. Emmeline glanced at Archie, then Grandfather, trying to keep the hopelessness from showing.

"May I make a phone call? In private." Jainey asked George, who promptly stood and led her into the den where he closed the doors, giving her privacy.

"You think she's calling my parents to bring me to an insane asylum?"

Archie rubbed her back.

Jainey returned to the kitchen with a sort of confidence on her face, though still unreadable to Emmeline. "We should get going," Jainey said to her sister. Emmy slouched in the chair, giving up all hope of getting her sister to believe them.

"Who did you call?" Emmeline asked after a good ten minutes of silence in the car.

"Em, you need to be careful."

"Of what?" She was curious as to *which* threat her sister was talking about.

"Just ... be careful."

Emmeline wanted to ask again who was on the phone; to drill Jainey like she would do to Emmeline, but she felt the tension radiating through her sister and didn't want to push.

"Thanks for trying." Emmeline closed the car door and walked inside, not meaning for it to come out as cold and satire as it did.

In the following days, Jainey went back to teasing Emmeline, as if the crazy information floated over her head. George and Archie continued caution when going into public, making sure to leave the house only when necessary, and not speaking to anyone. Judy was nowhere to be seen at church on Sunday, all but confirming the heartbreaking truth for Emmeline that the woman wasn't to be trusted.

"I still held hope," she said while walking out of the church with Archie.

He squeezed her hand and pressed his lips to it. "Will your parents let you come for the day if I promise to have you home right after dinner?"

She looked to her mother who seemed to be giving them a twitchy side-eye.

"Be right back." Emmeline ran to her sister and pulled her aside.

"The demons chasing you?"

Em rolled her eyes. "Can you cover for me so I can go to Archie's?"

Jainey waggled her eyebrows.

"*Stop*," the girl grinned, cheeks burning. "Mom clearly

47

hates him. If she thought you and I were going somewhere, I could sneak off and you can do … whatever it is you do." She waved her hand around.

Jainey looked to the ceiling and tilted her head in a side-to-side rhythm, considering the request. "Fine. We'll tell them we're headed to the movies, then dinner. That'll give us both hours away from the Neck Breathers."

"Perfect." Emmeline went back to Archie and told him and Grandfather to park around the corner of the church. Maud protested slightly at the girls leaving that moment, but Jainey pleaded, almost in a singsong voice, and their mother caved.

"I'll pick you up at seven p.m.," Jainey said as she pulled her car in front of Grandfather's.

"I really appreciate it, Jainey." Em unbuckled and hugged her sister, then joined the men.

- ⚬ঙ৺৹•৻৲৺৹ -

"The Proclaimers," Archie said, placing a CD in the player. "Best band in existence." He held up a wooden spoon like a microphone and sang *500 Miles* to his wife, giving Grandfather and Emmeline some entertainment as the golden afternoon sun shone in.

"It feels like we're already home when I'm with you both," Emmeline said in a daydreamy voice. "Even dressed like this, and Arch serenading me like *that*," she cackled.

"Well, you are home with us, dear," Grandfather patted her hand before standing. "I'll start supper." He went to the kitchen, and Archie sat on the couch, sliding his fingers in hers.

"I've been talking to Grandfather about home," he began, clearing his throat. "Emmy, what if we stayed?"

She pulled her hand away. "Stay?"

"We have so much more here - better chances at everything."

"Except living, if the Feared sink their claws into us."

"Exactly what I'm saying."

Emmeline held up her hands, perplexed by what he meant.

"Instead of looking for a way to go back, we need to put all of our energy into destroying them."

Emmeline looked away and gritted her teeth. "And Uncle Allistair?" She glanced back. "Shall I never see him again?"

Archie sighed. "I think it's the smartest choice at this point."

"So, no. No Uncle Allistair. Got it." Emmeline crossed her arms, her skin hot with fury. "Grandfather feels the same?"

"He said he'd support my decision."

"He was healthy back then, Arch. No bum leg, and Uncle Allistair and he grew close." She saw Grandfather attempting to give them privacy from the kitchen, but he glanced over his shoulder with droopy eyes.

"I'm trying to do what's best for us, Emmy."

"No, Archibald." She pointed a finger at him. "You're trying to do what's easiest for *you*."

Archie dropped his mouth to speak in defense, only nothing seemed to come out but an expression of shock.

Emmeline left the couch. "You do this often, you know. If things get tough and there's no straight answer, you run. What if your tenants disappointed you, Lord Emsworth, huh?" Emmeline felt her stomach burn, but she couldn't stop. "If the crops went bad, or if … if the damned plague hit, would you flee to another country where you think everything is perfect? Where nothing scares you?"

"And what about you? Always making the plans and never including me in the decisions?"

"I figured if you had an opinion, you'd share."

"Jesus, Emmeline. I didn't argue with you because they were unimportant matters. But this is bigger than both of us. You always think you know what's best, but it's my turn to do what's best for our family. Either we use this time to somehow go back a century, which seems hopeless since we have no leads, or we discover who the members of the Feared are, figure out how to wipe them out, then move to Scotland and buy land."

"And let your grandfather live forever with a bum leg?"

"At least he'll *live*. If we don't uncover these creatures soon, they will kill us. Then finding the portal would be for nothing."

"But I'll never see my uncle again. He raised me after my father …" she choked up.

"The cons of traveling back outweigh the pros." His voice was quiet, regretful, and final.

Emmeline clenched her hands into fists, then turned and left, slamming the door behind her. She knelt in the grass, letting out a wail. Tears of anger, sadness, and fear spilled down her face. She wished the emotions would wash away with them. "He's wrong," she snapped, panting in a frenzy.

He's not, her conscience argued. She slumped back.

Archie was right. She'd always dictated what would be done, thinking she knew best. She was controlling. She wiped her cheeks and rolled her eyes at herself, embarrassed that she wasn't even remotely aware enough to realize her husband's wants and needs differed from her own.

A slight rustle in the woods caught her attention.

"Em," Archie's voice was mellow behind her. She shifted, seeing his eyes red from crying. She leaped up and embraced him, kissed his cheek, and hugged him close. He buried his face in her neck.

"I'm so sorry," she whispered. "You're not the one who deserves my anger."

"Me too. We've been stressed, but we can't let this tear us apart."

She lifted his head and wiped his tears with her thumbs. "You think I'd run off just because of a little fight? Nah. I'm not so easily frightened."

He wrinkled his nose in an amused grin, then leaned down to kiss her, when a howl stunned them. From the caliginous woods stepped a wolf, big and gray, with teeth sharper than a rose's thorn, bigger than a bow's arrow. Emmeline stood in front of Archie, extending her arms and pushing him backward. She knew he had frozen with fear. The wolf approached the couple, stopping five feet away, then stared. Archie took Em's arms and tried pulling her into the safety of the house, but she stopped him.

"Wait, he won't hurt us," Emmeline swallowed at the words. "I can tell." She moved forward.

"What are you doing!"

She looked back at her husband. "It's okay." Then she inched toward the giant wolf, whose large paws sunk into the earth. The wolf lifted his head to meet her shaking, outstretched hand. As she brushed his fur, her body relaxed.

"Come here," she coaxed Archie, who was apprehensive. She called him over again, and, though hesitant, he walked sluggishly to her.

"You can pet him," Emmeline said.

He looked from the wolf's big eyes to Em's, who took his hand and placed it on the wolf's neck. Archie flinched, but the animal leaned into him, enjoying the massage.

"How?" he asked, scratching it behind the ear.

"I can hear his thoughts, sort of. They aren't words, but I can feel his emotions." Emmeline rubbed his underbelly. "He's here to protect us for the night."

Archie cast his glance at her, but the wolf dashed into the woods as a car pulled into the gravel driveway.

"What are you weirdos doing?" Jainey called out the window. She was early.

Emmeline approached her and said in a hushed voice, "Want me to be your servant for the next month?"

Chapter 10

"Jainey will tell them I ate some bad mozzarella sticks and went to bed," Emmeline told Grandfather and Archie after she and her sister spoke outside. "I'll be suffering for a while, doing her laundry and cleaning moldy dishes from under her bed, but it's worth it." She peeled a potato as Grandfather slid a pan of chicken into the oven. She knew that if her parents found out, they would skewer her, but she was sick of treating her relationship with her husband like it was a high school fling. And high school - she hated it with a passion now.

・☆ ⊱✧⊰ ☆ ・

Snuggled up to Archie warmed her, not only physically, but her heart was happy. She felt safe, protected, for the first night since all the truth came out. She could still feel the wolf's presence outside, calming any other fears residing in her heart.

"We have knowledge that we can take back with us … stuff that can help our people," she said as he clicked off the light. "It won't be the same, but just think of the difference we can make."

"I never thought about it that way." Archie pulled her closer.

"That's why I'm your better half," she teased, poking him in the side. "I have the best idea." Emmeline sat halfway up and brushed the hair from his face. "We'll add a bard to our list of hires, and you can teach him The Proclaimers songs."

"I love you," he whispered.

- ⚬ ⚬ ❀ ✦ ❀ ⚬ ⚬ -

"No school for Emmy today?" Archie handed her a mug full of iced tea the next morning.

She pushed her bedhead hair out of her face and plopped down at the table with a dreamy look. "I have the best husband ever."

"You're not wrong." He sat next to her, slid her chair closer to his, and filled the gap between their lips, hers parting in a smile when he put a warm hand on her cheek.

"Ah, now it feels like home," Grandfather said, jolting the two apart in surprise. "No, no, don't stop on my account. I'm off to run errands, so I'll leave you two newlyweds to your canoodling."

Emmeline's cheeks pinkened, lifting in an almost embarrassed smile.

"Be careful out there," Archie said. George tipped his hat to them and left.

"Let's celebrate." Archie jumped up and took her hands.

"Celebrate what?"

"Our honeymoon." He pulled her off the chair and lifted her up, spinning her around, then pressed his lips to hers again. When her feet were firm on the floor, he pulled something from his pocket, took her left hand, and slid on a silver band. "You'll need to take it off when you're at home, but I felt it was only right that my wife had a ring."

Emmeline wiped a tear from her face and rested her head on his shoulder, weaving her fingers through his, which also had a wedding band. If she had the choice, she'd never leave his arms.

"Come on, I want to take you somewhere."

- ⚔ ⚔ ⚔ -

"This makes my home sickness easier to bear." Emmeline intertwined her arms around his, skipping forward, when she saw the stable.

"Do you remember how to ride?"

"Do *you* remember how?" she countered. "As I recall, you were never very good."

"First of all, horses are tall. Second, you're only insulting yourself since you're the one who taught me."

Emmeline touched his cheek and kissed him. "You're a pure equestrian, Sweetpea."

"Yeah, yeah. Let's go, you comedian."

They mounted two beautiful Clydesdales and took a trail through the forest. Em inhaled the air and took in every sight - the squirrels jumping from branch to branch, birds fluttering around their nests, the autumn leaves starting to fall. It felt like Scotland - like she and Archie were out on their daily ride, enjoying each other's company.

"What's wrong?" Archie asked when he saw her

melancholy expression.

"I miss this. I miss it so much."

He pulled on the reins, halting the horse. "Emmeline, if I have to claw my way through time itself, I will take you home. Nights like that and days like this will be ours again. No repercussions, no fears - just us."

"How was I fortunate enough to find you, not just once, but twice?" She took in every inch of his face, although she could sketch him from memory down to the last freckle. This man was more handsome than anyone she'd ever seen, and he was all hers. He was able to tell her he loved her just by the look on his gentle face.

His expression turned intense when an ungodly screech came from behind them.

"Em, *run*," Archie shouted. Without asking why, she took off. She glanced at Archie as he gave his horse a nudge and followed right after.

Behind them, a hooded person was galloping closer, leaning forward and viciously kicking his horse's side. Emmeline couldn't see his face beyond a prickly chin and his teeth, which were bared down in a wild smile.

"Keep going, no matter what! Do you understand?" Archie told her while his horse gained speed behind hers. She directed Remie, her horse, to go faster, rounding a corner to evade the assailant. She heard the sound of her Remie's hooves, but no others.

"Whoa," she said, slowing the animal to a stop. Archie was no longer behind her. She cursed and turned the horse around. She made it to the other path and saw Archie on the ground, fighting the hooded man off him.

Emmeline screamed in anger as the man punched her husband in the stomach, causing him to curl up and cough. Remie barreled at the man, though Emmeline couldn't recall commanding the horse forward. Remie reared, clocking the man in the face, knocking him unconscious. He fell to the ground, and his hood fell back. Emmeline jumped down, dropping beside Archie who had mostly caught his breath. She helped him sit up, and they both looked at the man sprawled before them.

"Do you recognize him?" Archie asked.

She shook her head, trying to calm herself. The horse snorted behind them.

"Thank you." She rubbed the side of Remie's face. When she looked into his eyes, she was stunned to hear something - not quite words - enter her brain.

"I … I think he just spoke to me," Emmeline said.

"The horse?"

She nodded. "Like the wolf. Can you understand me?" she asked the horse, to which he replied with a gentle nudge to Em's face. She hugged Remie.

"You drive," Archie said to her, but looked back at the man.

"Your horse," Emmeline paused her sentence, scanned the area, realizing Archie's horse, and the cloaked man's, had run off.

Can you find them? She thought, peering into the horse's eyes. He snorted.

Remie trotted along the trail, seeming to gaze around the woods just as Archie and Emmeline were doing.

"Maybe we should take Remie home to be our

protector," Emmeline joked, though her tone faltered with a tinge of fear.

"There," Archie exclaimed. Two horses stomped the dirt, upset. Em jumped down and took both of their reins, calming them in a hushed voice.

"Their feelings, I can nearly hear them." She walked the two back to Remie and Archie. "They're terrified. Evil and demon, those are the words that keep flashing in my mind."

"The Feared."

Chapter 11

"Emmeline, breakfast," Maud called up the stairs the next morning. Emmeline had successfully convinced her mom she'd arrived home from school after the horse ride.

When the girl entered the kitchen filled with the aroma of bacon and sausage, her mom tilted her head. "Where's your ring?"

"What?" Emmeline took a biscuit and furrowed her brow, knowing she had been diligent in taking her wedding ring off before coming home.

"I don't know." Maud huffed out a laugh. "I had a dream that you were married."

Emmeline straightened.

"No more chocolate before bed for you," Joe said from the stove where he scrambled his infamous cheese and ham eggs. He gave his wife a wink. Maud spread jam on her biscuit when Jainey came dancing into the kitchen singing a Backstreet Boys' song.

"You have a beautiful voice." Their mother seemed astonished. The girls stared at her. She shook her head and said, "I mean, you always have had a lovely set of vocals. Just today you sound especially good." She took a sip of coffee and looked at her plate. Emmeline couldn't help but notice the confusion in her mom's eyes.

"Oh, Honey," Joe addressed his wife. "I forgot to tell

you that I found a nice little farm stand on my way home from work Friday. They have homemade wine. Jainey and I will swing by Emmeline's school after work, and we'll pick out a few bottles for you. I feel like I haven't seen my daughters in ages." Joe said, kissing each girl on the head.

Emmeline had planned to skip school once again and spend time with Archie, but she'd have to make it back by the end of the day, so her father didn't find out.

- ❦ -

"We got another note this morning," Archie said, sliding the paper across the table.

> *Bother not with your research. The ability to time travel is not in the realm of possibilities for you.*

"Oh crap."

"They know what we've been up to." Grandfather had his hands submerged in soapy water.

Archie rubbed the back of his neck.

"We'll figure it out. Please don't back out," Emmeline said.

He blew air out and nodded. "They don't call us the Fearless for nothing."

"Who's this *they*?" Emmeline chortled.

"Tell me about the cloaked man," Grandfather George wiped down a plate he'd just washed. "You say you didn't recognize him?"

Em squeezed her eyes shut. "I want to say I did, I don't

know if my mind is playing tricks on me. He seems familiar the more I think about it."

"Think hard, my dear. Is it a man you see around here? Maybe at your school?"

"I never thought about suspecting anyone at school. If the Feared are trying to surround us by gaining entry into our lives, it would only make sense that a teacher or student is part of them."

"Would you two be comfortable going back to the school - Emmeline attends her classes, and Archibald, you could act as if you're touring the school."

"It's not a bad idea, providing our minds don't get wiped." Emmeline took her bag and agreed. If they could find out who each member of the Feared was, they could take them out, then go home.

- ·⊗·⊙·⊗·⊙· -

"Glad to have you back in class, Emmeline. Must've been some sickness," the English teacher remarked when Emmeline came in late.

Yeah, you're on my list, now, lady, Em thought to herself. Archie was able to get a visitor's pass. He would take a look around, and Emmeline would attend the rest of her classes, scrutinizing every single person.

"Anything?" Archie asked when the two met up at the end of the school day.

"Some teachers were rude, probably because I haven't done homework in weeks, but other than that no one stood out. Anyways, Dad will be here any minute. I'll call you tonight." She gave him a long goodbye kiss and moved to leave.

"More," he said, pulling her back, kissing her again. She giggled against his lips.

"Alright Romeo, I gotta go."

- ⚬⚬⚬⚬✦⚬⚬⚬⚬ -

"Afternoon." The man behind a large wine stand tipped his hat to the girls and their father as they made their way up the dirt driveway. The bottles of red and white wine sat in their own slots on a box of individual cubbies, laying at a tilt in some hay. Their labels were decorated with fancy flourishes. Even Em wanted to keep a bottle just because it was beautiful, though she did fancy a glass on occasion during banquets back home. She looked around the property as her dad picked out a few bottles. A barn stood in the back, its open doors showing off large machines and barrels inside. The white house with a wrap-around porch was over to the right. The trees scattered around the fields were full of orange and red leaves, as if they were on fire.

"Ready, girls?" Joe spoke to Jainey about their annual work meeting tomorrow as he drove the car away from the big house. Em wished her sister would heed her warning about Geoffrey.

"Why don't I take you two for dinner," Joe interrupted her thoughts. She'd feel terrible saying no. Her dad seemed to be enjoying their company, so she agreed, though plagued with the thought of the Feared being in town ready to attack.

Chapter 12

"This is ridiculous." Maud furiously chopped carrots for dinner the next day.

"I think Mr. Armack was exaggerating," Emmeline said about the school janitor she'd decided to follow around.

"Emmeline, you knocked him to the floor and sprained his wrist. You're damn lucky he's not pressing charges." Maud pointed a spoon at her. "What you were doing somersaulting across the computer lab I can't imagine."

Emmeline held in a snicker. She may have gotten a little too into spy mode. Archie and George cleared Mr. Armack from the suspect list after that.

Maud continued raving about Emmeline's failing grades and how she's been skipping school.

"I'm not an imbecile." Maud slammed a pot of water on the stove, dropped the carrots in, splashing some water out, and wrenched the burner knob to the highest setting. "George Emsworth clearly knows about you running around with his grandson, so he must not care enough about you or your education."

"That's not true," Emmeline argued.

"I'm at the end of my rope, and if it snaps, you better watch it." Maud popped a cork and poured a glass of wine from the farmstand.

Em was speechless. Had her mother gone mad? "I'm

going to bed. My stomach hurts."

"Oh, now you're sick? Don't bet on staying home from school tomorrow. And I'll be calling to ensure that you're there."

Emmeline slipped away, hoping not to catch another glare from her mom.

"After tonight, I'm not so sure my mom isn't one of them," she said to Archie on the phone.

"I can see why she'd be mad, not knowing what's really going on."

"Arch, *mad* doesn't cover how she acted tonight. Anyway, I checked out the UPS guy today. Turns out our neighbor just really likes online shopping."

"Off the list he goes," Archie said. So far, the list was filled with smudges, crossed-off names, and erased pencil marks. Only three names remained: Judy, Geoffrey, and Anonymous from the trail ride.

"Dad's been golfing with Geoffrey, so I lock myself in my room when he comes to pick him up. He seems to insist on driving."

"And Jainey still won't listen to you about him?"

"Nope."

- ·❀❧·❁❦·❀❧· -

Jainey set the mail on the table when she came in from work the next evening. Emmeline inspected her sister's actions, as she did on a nightly basis, to see if there were any suspicious changes.

"Wanna take a picture?" Jainey said when she caught

her sister staring.

"Of your ugly mug?" Em chortled and lifted the glass of water to her mouth when the front page of the newspaper caught her eye. In the black and white photograph, an old man dressed in early 1800s clothing stood in front of a house with a wrap-around porch and a barn in the back. A second photograph to the right showed the same house and barn, only in absolute ruins.

Early last week, on October 19th of 1999, a fire destroyed one of Monmouth's historical properties. Built in 1803, Maetree Farm was the top supplier of dairy goods for the town.

She read the headline, then snatched up the paper as her mouth fell open. She tapped the picture and attempted to speak, though her words were choppy. "This … this is the house," she began.

"What are you jabbering about?" Jainey said.

"That *house*, the farm we were at a couple days ago! It burned down last week."

Her older sister rolled her eyes and leaned over to look. Her attitude-riddled face dropped. "It *is*," she marveled, then looked at her sister, eyes expanding.

"Nonsense, how could it be?" Their father took a look. "Every farmhouse around here looks similar."

Em cleared her throat. "Do you guys mind if I head to Archie's right now, I have to …"

Joe cut her short with an exasperated sigh. "Can't we just spend one night together as a family?"

She bit her lip. She was almost certain her family was

bewitched to think the farmhouse was really there, kind of like Archie and Grandfather's mind swipe, and she wanted to let them know.

"I'll be back before eight, I promise."

"Not tonight," Maud said from her chair in the living room. She placed her lips to the glass of wine and sipped.

Emmeline, tongue in cheek, paused to regain patience. It'd been a hard few months to follow rules set by people who thought of her as "just a teen".

"It's important," she sort of growled through clenched teeth.

Her mother shot a look and boomed with an authoritative voice, "You spend entirely too much time with that boy, Emmeline. You need some separation. A week." She took another drink.

Emmy shook her leg as she considered the consequences of what she was about to do. "Sorry, Mom, but no. I'll be back." She grabbed Jainey's keys, knowing the consequences of that would be severe, as well.

Maud yelled after her, but Em slammed the door, ran to the car, and drove off before anyone could stop her.

- ⚬⚬⚭⚬⚭⚬⚭⚬ -

"Mom's angry … again," she said, taking off her coat and telling Archie what happened and about the farm.

Grandfather came into the room holding a novel. "Sit, kids. I found something pertaining to our journey home."

"Hold on." Emmeline closed the shades and made sure the door was bolted. "Okay."

George opened his book and flipped the pages. "This tells us almost everything we need to know about traveling back."

"Blood Moon?" Archie read the title, then flipped the book over to scan the description. "Grandfather, this is a novel about vampires."

"The one about the Feared was supposedly fantasy, and yet …" Emmeline raised her brow and motioned to the door.

"Well, what makes this one different from the books we've been searching through for the past couple months?" Archie seemed exasperated. Emmeline placed a hand on his knee, knowing he was losing hope.

George looked at the couple. "This one was left on our doorstep."

Emmeline's mouth opened. "Who would …"

"I'm not sure, but it seems we may have someone on our side."

"Why haven't they shown themselves?"

"It's probably a trap," Archie said. The three of them sat quietly, each one debating what the truth was.

"The book tells the tale of a total lunar eclipse, how it opens many realms, and all magic is possible under it," Grandfather said.

"We could be waiting months for an eclipse to happen." Archie ran a shaking hand through his hair. "And even then, we won't know if it'll be a total eclipse until that night."

Grandfather pulled a folded paper from the back of the book, hope in his eyes while handing it to Emmeline.

She unfolded it and read, "All Hallow's Eve."

"I want to know who left this." Archie stood.

"My dear boy, our options are limited."

"Grandfather's right." Emmeline walked to Archie and took his hands. "This is our only lead on getting home. Will you try?"

He stroked her cheek, then nodded. "It's tomorrow, Halloween. The Feared surely know about the portal if *we* do."

"Yes. That means they'll try to attack before we have the chance to escape," George remarked.

"Does this portal just pop open or something?" Archie asked.

Emmeline cursed and turned to George. "Does it say anything about a location?"

George shook his head. "I would gamble that whoever gave this to us will reveal themselves in the near future. For now, we wait."

Chapter 13

"This is unacceptable behavior." Maud and Joe stood in front of Emmeline after she returned home.

"I'm not trying to disrespect you and your rules, but there's a reason I've been skipping school and running off. Some serious stuff is happening, and I think it's time I tell you."

Joe sat at the kitchen table and coaxed Maud to join him when she didn't budge from her stiff stance in front of Emmeline.

The girl took a deep breath and joined her parents. "We're in danger."

"What are you talking ab ..."

"Something is after us, Archie and me. The truth is, I'm not really from here. I was born into a noble family over a thousand years ago. Archie and I were married. These creatures called the Feared attacked us, but we somehow escaped to the future. They followed us."

"Enough." Maud stood. "That boy is clearly bad news. He's made her crazy," she said to her husband, pointing at Emmy.

"Maud, let's hear her out."

She took a sip of the wine on the table.

"Tomorrow is Halloween. A blood moon will open a portal, giving us the chance to get back to the tenth century where we came from, and we've decided to do it. We want you to come with us."

They sat in silence. Maud looked outraged, but Joe was calm, his expression unreadable.

"What's that?" Joe pointed to the book in her hand.

"Just a book."

"Emmeline, go to your room. Your father and I need to talk." Maud tapped the stem of the glass with nails as red as the wine.

"But this is …"

"Your mother is right. Go on." Joe nodded to the stairs.

— ⚘ —

Two long hours passed while Em paced her room, going over potential conversations she could have with her parents that would convince them she was telling the truth. She glanced at her desk where a photo of Archie sat, recalling his pleading for her to stay with him earlier that night.

"It's time to tell them," she'd said to Archie before going back to her house. "You and I will be home by tomorrow, but my family has to come with us." She kissed him, then waved goodbye from her car. The fear in his eyes as she walked out the door gave her a shiver.

She reached for the phone to let him know she was okay when her father called her downstairs. She galloped down with every hope her parents would ask her for more details, signaling that they trusted her.

"This is our friend, Melianna," Maud said when Em

came around the corner. "She's a renowned therapist. We think she can help you and your ..."

Joe took Maud's hand, stopping her from whatever vile insult she was about to throw at her daughter.

The blonde stepped forward. "Hello, Emmeline."

The girl greeted her with a handshake, silently coming up with a plan to get out of this. She'd need to figure out a way to get her family to the portal. Clearly, they wouldn't come to terms in a day.

Melianna sat on the couch. "Your parents told me some interesting things."

"I'm sure they did."

The phone rang. Her mother picked up and told the person not to call again. *Archie*.

"I've read that one," the therapist said, pointing to the book about the blood moon in the girl's hands. Em wanted to read it so she'd know exactly what Grandfather had been talking about but didn't realize she'd been clutching it like a stress ball since she returned.

"This book is about time travel and star-crossed lovers. Perhaps you're projecting the life of the couple in the book with your own relationship. Emmeline, I think you may have reality mixed up with fantasy."

"I definitely don't." How long was this session of mouse crap going to last?

The therapist slowly nodded. She then stood and approached Joe and Maud. "I believe Emmeline needs some alone time. Maybe this Archie fellow isn't bad, but you said she started acting up when she met him? Yes, I think time away from the boy is wise. No contact for a few days. And no fantasy novels."

"Who the hell are you to boss me around? We met literally ten minutes ago."

"*Emmeline*," Joe scolded.

"It's alright, Joe. We can meet again in a few days if you like." Melianna took her leave, saying the family should discuss what happens moving forward. Maud left the room for a few minutes. She came back with Emmeline's telephone.

"Are you insane?" She marched to her mother, who put a hand out.

"No, but I'm beginning to think *you* are."

"Things have gone too far, Hun." Joe put a hand on his daughter's shoulder, but she shrugged it off. He lifted his chin. "Archibald will be staying away. This relationship is … I don't even have words for it."

"You can't keep me from him. He and I are married."

"Show us the marriage certificate." Joe crossed his arms, waiting expectantly. "Nothing? Go to your room."

Emmeline eyed the door but saw that the three sets of keys were gone. She went upstairs while hot, angry tears rolled down her face. She washed them away in the bathroom, but she'd let herself get so upset she wretched in the toilet. She sat on the cold, bathroom floor breathing deeply to stop her stomach from churning.

She couldn't escape from her second-story window, and she had no way to contact Archie. She sprawled out on her comforter, her mind spinning. Demonic fae, time travel, and now crazy-overprotective parents made her thoughts ambush her in every way possible.

Her rumbling stomach urged her to leave her bedroom the next morning. She peeked into Jainey's room, hoping to talk to someone sane. Her bed was made, which she never did. No crumpled papers covered her desk, and dirty laundry wasn't scattered about the carpet.

Something wasn't right. Jainey never tidied up, even when their mom threatened to ground her. Emmy looked around the room again, realizing all of Jainey's boy band posters and CDs were missing, too.

Heart hammering out of her chest, Emmeline ran downstairs to find Maud sitting at the table.

"Where's Jainey?" Emmeline didn't want to talk to her mom but *had* to talk to her sister.

"Who?"

Emmeline stumbled back, then noticed the glass of wine in the woman's hands, and a half-empty bottle on the table. That wine, it had to be enchanted.

"He's a fae, that wine dealer."

Maud tilted her head. Emmeline made a split decision and grabbed the wine glass and bottle, throwing them into the sink, splattering red liquid and glass all over. Maud slammed her chair across the room and grabbed the girl by her neck.

"*Mom*," she gasped as the woman squeezed Em's throat.

Emmeline moved her hand around the counter to find anything she could defend herself with. Her vision hazed over in a pink hue as her hand made contact with a large piece of the wine bottle. She jammed it into Maud's back as hard as she could. Her mother released Em and stumbled back, wailing. The girl ran out the door. She coughed and staggered but didn't slow her pace. She only knew she had to get as far from the house as possible.

A car screeched to a halt, and someone grabbed her. She kicked and pounded her fists on the person's chest.

"Emmeline, stop!" Archie's voice fought through the beating in her ears.

Her vision cleared enough to see his crystal eyes staring down at her. She cried out, falling into his arms. He picked her up and put her in the front seat, taking her to his house before asking any questions.

Emmeline laid on the couch with a cold cloth pressed to her forehead. Archie's warm hand squeezed hers. She could feel it shaking with worry as she recovered enough to relay what had happened.

"You're staying here," he said, grazing his hand over her hair.

She licked her dry lips. "I need to find my sister."

Chapter 14

"The therapist," Emmeline spoke with a raspy voice, then sipped the hot tea Archie handed her. She cleared her throat as best she could. "She only talked to me for five minutes, then demanded you be removed from my life, essentially. She wanted us separated."

"Have you ever seen her before?"

"No, but apparently she's friends with my parents, so she wormed her way into my life."

"What's her name?" Archie took a pencil, ready to write the therapist on their suspect list.

"Melianna. Not sure of her last name." Em looked around the sunny living room. "Where's Grandfather?"

"I don't know. He must have left early this morning."

"Oh my God, they got him!" She jumped from the couch, spilling the tea on the carpet.

"No, Em." He embraced her, calming her shaking body. "He left a note saying he'd be back. He's okay."

She wasn't convinced but agreed to Archie's suggestion of resting. She laid, wrapped in a blanket, and cuddled in his arms as he clicked on the tv.

"... from prison months ago and was found early this morning in an old hunting shack. The perpetrator has not been found as of yet, but investigators are hopeful. Back to you, Regina."

A photo of the escaped criminal was shown on the tv, along with the location her body was found, though this morning the "hunting shack" resembled the American dream house.

"*Arch*," Emmeline cried out. "That's my mom, it's Maud! That's my house!"

The front door slammed open. Emmeline's throat burned as she screamed, nearly knocking Archie off the couch.

"Quickly, children. We must go," Grandfather said, then hobbled back to his car. Archie and Emmeline stayed put on the couch, trying to process the news and Grandfather's abrupt intrusion.

"*Now!*" they heard him yell from outside.

"What's the matter?" Archie asked while Grandfather drove ten over the speed limit. George said nothing as he focused on the winding road. He pulled into a driveway and honked the horn. Geoffrey emerged from the house.

"It's time," George called to the man.

"Grandfather, are you mad?! He's with *them*." Archie and Emmeline's faces were wide with shock as the bank man climbed into the front seat.

"Geoffrey is not our enemy, my dear boy." He backed the car down the driveway and took off again.

"Tell us what's happening," Emmeline demanded, her throat feeling better, but her stomach still agitated.

"This morning, I saw the Feared in their true form."

"It's All Hallow's Eve, the one day they cannot hide themselves - er, they cannot hide themselves to those who know about them, that is." The bank man looked in the back seat.

"Where'd you see them?" Emmeline asked.

George glanced in the rearview mirror with sad eyes. "I went down to that farmstand to check out the owner you told me about, but as I pulled in, two creatures stood talking. I could tell who they were, though they had a few different features from their human selves."

"So is the owner one of them?"

"Yes, but so is the man you know as your father. Joseph Foster is not human."

Archie took Emmeline's stiff hand, and she shook her head in a slow sweep of denial.

"They saw me and realized I could see their true form. They came for me, but I was able to get away."

"What's the plan? Where are we going?" Archie asked.

"To sacred ground, where we have the advantage to harvest the powers residing there," Geoffrey said.

Chapter 15

"An old factory?" Emmeline wrinkled her nose as the car pulled into an empty lot overgrown with tall grass and weeds. A few dead trees lined the front of the building which was covered in brown vines. She stared at the shattered windows and moldy, rotten doors.

"We'll head to the warehouse basement. I'll be able to charge my powers from the dirt floor." The bank man stepped from the vehicle, the others following.

Archie and Geoffrey pulled open the plywood nailed to the door. Em stayed in a silent shock as the bank man conjured a ball of light to illuminate the stairs to the basement. It was a vast room with shelves of old boxes. Plenty of hiding spaces.

"Alright, I need some answers." Emmeline swung around, peering directly at the strange magician. Grandfather pointed Archie to a few chairs. Once they were seated in a circle, Geoffrey nodded at Emmeline.

"First off, who are you?"

"I am a descendant of Lord Allistair Caliburn, the greatest wizard to ever live. The gift of magic has been passed down for generations … down to me."

"When Lord Allistair learned that you were missing, he didn't rest until he found you. He searched for days," Grandfather added. "He discovered you both clinging to your lives as the fae fed on your souls."

Archie looked as sick as Emmy felt.

"Those creatures put up a good fight, but in the end, Allistair won, sending the Feared fleeing, though they never stopped terrorizing the towns. He used every drop of magic left in him to send you to the future – to this time – knowing as long as those evil things were out there, you wouldn't be safe where you were."

"We were reborn." Archie rubbed his temple.

Grandfather shook his head. "Your memories of your childhood in this century are false. They never happened."

"*What*?" Emmeline raised her brow.

"Like I said, Allistair was powerful," Geoffrey said.

"How do you know all of this?" Archie asked.

"Legends of the great wizard were passed down in my family. Many of them, specifically those who never possessed the gift, believed they were nothing but bedtime stories. My grandmother, who had magic, knew the truth. She taught me to tap into my own powers. She passed away last year. Before she went, she told me of your arrival. I was to be one of your protectors. I was to fight alongside you."

Emmeline opened her mouth to speak when a screech echoed through the rising moonlit windows above the ground, shaking the building and dislodging bricks and debris. Archie stood, but Geoffrey grabbed his shoulder.

"They are the Feared. You can't defeat them with some snide comments and karate moves." Geoffrey looked at the dust falling from the ceiling. "They will have a tough time entering this place, and I sense they're not all here yet. They won't dare attack without full force."

"Why can't they enter?" Emmeline fidgeted. "What's so special about this place?"

"My family owned this factory - Caliburn knives."

"And it's a powerful place because you're a family of wizards. Makes sense," Em said.

"Grandfather, you said our memories here were false, how long have we been here? What's real?" Archie shifted in the cold, metal chair.

"I'd say about six months."

"Did you know?"

"Not until I met Geoffrey." George adjusted his bad leg. "I followed him for a few days to see if our suspicions were correct. He finally confronted me."

"Why didn't the fae kill us the moment they arrived?"

"Ah, a good question. I had the same one." Geoffrey looked at the boy. "Time travel is the most considerable magic out there. They followed you here, so their powers were depleted. They needed time to regain, but, unfortunately for them, you and Emmeline found each other rather quickly. That's why they disguised themselves as people around you. They wanted to try to prevent you from being together."

"Power weakened or not, it isn't hard to kill humans," Emmeline said.

"You are no human."

"Say what now?"

The young wizard turned to the girl and took a deep breath, exhaling slowly. "You are not Lord Allistair's ward, nor his niece. You're his daughter."

The breath caught in her throat.

"Allistair didn't want you to know he was your father. He worried that if you got too close, you'd find out what he really was … a wizard. This information could attach you to the dangers he constantly faced. This is why he placed you in the home of his brother."

Archie rubbed one of his eyes. "You're saying Emmeline has magic."

"Yes. That's why those fae haven't killed her." The wizard nodded to the ceiling. "I can sense your wife's powers."

"I'm relieved," Grandfather said. "It means we have a chance, kids. We have a very good chance."

A dark, harmonious chanting rang through the room, interrupting the conversation.

Geoffrey walked to a small window at the top of the room. "They're ready."

Chapter 16

"How many do you think there are?" Emmeline and Archie stood as well.

"Plenty."

The sound of glass shattering and wood splintering came from above. Archie wrapped his arms around Emmeline and kissed her hair as his eyes darted to each corner of the room. The basement reverberated with the chanting, which had grown louder, and more fierce.

"We need to find a place to hide," Emmeline said, looking from shelf to shelf. "Especially Grandfather."

Archie agreed.

"I hate to be useless," George said, propping himself up with the cane, his leg seeming to bother him more than usual.

"You haven't been." Emmeline took his free hand and helped him to a darker area where he could hide in the shadows.

A force blasted through the stone wall across the warehouse. Candles appeared and ignited, giving an eerie glow. An enormous dark fae stepped into the light, followed by a large group of hooded beings.

"Good evening, daughter," it growled.

"*Joe.*" Archie clenched his fists.

Though she was shaking from head to toe, Emmeline

dared to move forward. "You are *not* my father, beast."

The creature clicked his tongue. "Aw, do you not remember me? Well, it's understandable, I suppose. I have changed my appearance a bit." He motioned to his body, the wings, leathery skin, and sharp teeth.

"Yeah, I know who you are."

"I am not talking of being your father here, stupid girl."

It was then that Emmeline remembered. Lord Joseph Caliburn, brother of Allistair, and the man she had called father a thousand years ago.

"Are you *kidding* me?" she screamed, overwhelmed with anger. She was sick of the secrets, and though a group of sadistic barbarians stood before her, she thought of another lie. "Allistair told me you were killed in the war."

"Now that's insulting. I worked for years to be where I am now, and my brother has never been proud of my accomplishments." His words were glazed with sarcasm.

"What'd you do, sell your soul?" She flared her nostrils.

"I promised my soul to the king of dark fae, but then I took his."

Emmeline grimaced as his eyes cut through her, his pupils becoming serpent-like slits. He hissed, and Emmy stumbled back, though they were at least ten yards away from each other.

"They can't touch you, Em." Archie stood next to her and placed a hand on her back.

"We may not be able to touch *her*," Joe started, "but without you, the prophecy will be broken. And trust me boy … we can touch you."

With that, his many companions lowered their hoods,

revealing their faces. Judy sneered at Emmeline, who was trying to catch her breath as the word *prophecy* ran through her mind. The Feared lifted their hands as one, preparing to do something detrimental, but a wave of power filled the air. It surrounded Emmeline and blinded the Feared.

"Get behind me," Geoffrey shouted, holding his palms toward the fae.

Archie obeyed, pulling Emmeline into his arms and running behind the wizard. Geoffrey's powers faltered, and the faes' wings ripped through their cloaks - spindly bones covered in feathers, wet with evil. Their skin was gray, and they bared sharp teeth. Joe whipped his hand toward Archie, but George pushed the boy out of the way and the impact hit him instead, throwing him off his feet.

"Grandfather," Archie and Emmeline screamed at once.

"Leave me, I'm fine." George sat up, holding his side. Geoffrey pushed his palms out, again sending a wall of ripples toward the Feared. The force protected them from the blows of the faes' attacks. Geoffrey gritted his teeth, his face turning red as he struggled to hold them off.

"George," Geoffrey called behind him. "Your cane, hold up your cane!"

The old man took the walking stick in his shaky hand and held it in the air. Geoffrey closed his eyes and uttered a spell, dividing his energy between the forcefield and the spell.

"Take me up," he boomed. "Cast me away." The cane wriggled, then emitted a flashing light. Grandfather sat on the floor with a sword - long, silver, and heavy - gleaming between the wrinkled fingers of the man's frail hand.

"To Archibald," Geoffrey demanded.

With an impressive, impossible burst of strength, George tossed the sword to his grandson. The wizard's wall vanished, though he pushed every muscle into preserving it. The winged creatures hissed and descended on the group, who scattered, using the shelves as barriers. Archie wielded the sword, slashing the air while the fae dodged him, laughing maliciously.

"Watch out," Emmeline yelled. Archie swung around. The sword collided with a wing, slicing it in half. The creature cried out - an ear-piercing, ungodly sound. The boy's mouth hung open, standing dumbfounded before he shook his head and refocused. He plunged his blade directly into the beast's heart.

- ❦ -

Black filled Archie's eyes – his ears. He could taste its glooming death. Dark, glittering smoke floated around the chaos, dancing before him. A raspy, outraged voice came from behind.

"You wield the stone sword." The Judy creature curled her lip, but there was a tint of fear in her shadowy eyes.

The sides of the boy's lips lifted. This sword brought hope. He took the weapon to war, connecting its hot metal to the cold flesh of the Feared, taking them out. Joe, king of the Feared, stood tall, seven feet in terrifying height. He threw his head back and gave a shrill screech, chilling every inch of Emmeline's skin. She was crouched in front of Grandfather, protecting him, knowing she couldn't be touched. Geoffrey and Archie held their defensive stances, waiting for the fae to attack. Joe whipped his hands around, his spells being deflected by Geoffrey's, his evil comrades falling into step. Archie raised his sword and sliced the nearly invisible balls of power the beast threw, while the wizard fought through clenched teeth.

Joe and the remaining fae halted and opened their mouths, inhaling the smoke and ashes of the fallen.

Geoffrey shot Archie a panicked look. "They're soaking up their powers, becoming stronger." He turned to Emmeline. "Call the animals."

"What?"

"Call them. They'll come."

"I don't know how!"

"Yes, you do." The wizard faced the remaining Feared again. It was an advantage to strike while they were busy. Geoffrey gave it his all, sending lightning, zaps, anything and everything he had left, but a forcefield had conjured around the dark creatures. "Emmeline," he pleaded.

Her body shook with fear and anger, seeing that Geoffrey was losing. Her heart felt a duty to this man - wizard. Geoffrey Caliburn was her family.

Emmeline thought about animals. Which ones? She remembered all the sunny days with Lord Allistair - how happy he was to teach her to care for the bees. He had thrown his head back, slapping his knee with a belly laugh when Emmeline came up with the name "Fuzzy Buzzies," and didn't call them by any other name after. Emmeline felt something triggered by the memory. She felt Grandfather's hand on hers, an encouragement to keep calling. The king fae and his minions were nearly done absorbing the energy, and Geoffrey was looking defeated, though he didn't stop fighting. Archie seemed to be losing momentum, too.

"Show me your powers, you piteous wizard. You're no match," Joseph growled at Geoffrey.

Joe slammed his hands into the wall, and a splintering echoed around the room. The ceiling cracked, dropping bits of drywall on their heads. The evil faery raised his arm to strike again when a swarm of bees rushed into the room through the windows, the cracks in the ceiling, and the busted wall, surrounding the beasts. They stung their faces – their mouths, their eyes. Joe swatted, crying out with fury, freeing his hand from the stinging army to produce a fireball so hot, so large that it incinerated half of the bees. The screams that came from the faes' gaping mouths sent a depression through the room.

Emmeline begged her mind to concentrate, though mourning the loss of her tiny army, trying to influence the rest of the bees, but she cried out in fear as the rest of the cloaked creatures rushed them. Archie grabbed her hand. Geoffrey delivered a forceful battle cry, as if this were the way he wanted to go; protecting his family was the only goal on his mind.

"Geoffrey, *stop*," Emmeline shrieked.

The shadows descended upon him. Em ran for him, Archie following close behind. A clawed hand grabbed Archie by the throat while another dragged Geoffrey across the gravel floor. The Feared had begun their feast on the wizard's soul when the whipping of vigorous wind blew the cellar door off its hinges, carrying with it a harmonious chorus of voices. The music swept around the room, knocking the dark fae off their feet. Emmeline's wails dried up; the muscles in her shaking body relaxed; the veil of death brightened as her sister stepped down the stairs.

Jainey's arms extended to welcome the elemental fusion of music engulfing the room. Her opera vocals of Celtic chants danced through Emmeline's ears. She was so mesmerized by the power glowing in Jainey's eyes that Em hadn't noticed what it did to the Feared. The beasts were plastered to the wall by the visible vibrations coming from her older sister's voice. She sang with emotions Emmeline had thought insignificant until this point. Her song was the warm sun after freezing weather. Her song was the smell of fresh rain. It was deer grazing in a field, and a white crescent moon shining against a violet sky. It was protection. It was *love*.

Chapter 17

The dark fae fought against Jainey's voice, but she sang louder with every move they made. Archie and Emmeline had carried Geoffrey's wounded body to the back of the room and laid him next to Grandfather, who clutched the wizard's hand. Archie squeezed the sword until his knuckles were white, ready for a battle.

Joe ground his sharp teeth, using every muscle in his body to fight against the music like it was a tornado holding him against the brick wall.

Emmeline couldn't help but smile in awe at her sister, who Em had thought didn't believe her. Now she was here conjuring musical magic. Emmeline's astonishment was cut short as she watched the being whom she'd known as a father for so long widening his primitive eyes, and in one swift move, he slashed the throats of every faerie in the room, inhaling the essence of the beings. It was exactly what Joseph needed to push against Jainey's power.

The dark king's eyes targeted Emmeline. He rushed her, swiping his hand toward Jainey, slapping her with a force so strong the music quieted, then to Archie, knocking the blade to the floor. Emmeline grabbed the sword. She swung at the monster, nicking his cheek. Darkness circled her, kicking Archie back to the ground as he yelled and lunged.

"What do you want?" Emmeline yelled as a swirling

blackness whipped her hair around. She couldn't find flesh to hit with the sword, only ash-filled wind. It isolated her, laughing insidiously as it circled her.

"Your child," a distant voice replied.

"I don't have a child." Emmeline turned, trying to catch a solid part of the creature.

"Save yourself the pain. Surrender to me now, and you will never know loss."

"Never know loss? I was raised to think you were my father for fourteen years. I thought I had lost you. Then I lost Allistair. My *real* dad tried saving me the pain of finding out what you really were - reprehensible, maggot-eating, soulless *TRASH*!"

A hiss came from the whirlwind.

"Because of you," she said as she swung the sword into the smoke. "I was taken from my life." She swung again. "You want my surrender, and I want your ashes to cover," *swing*, "this," *swing*, "floor!" *SWING*.

Emmeline's sword made contact, dispersing the smoke and wind, and sent Joe hurtling across the room, his right wing dangling, the thin bones broken. He snarled and leaped at her. Jainey's song began again, her voice gaining strength, becoming higher in pitch. The fae held his ears, squeezing his eyes closed and growling. Jainey strode toward him, her voice still raising. Finally, she lifted her arms, belting out the highest, most beautiful frequency Emmeline had ever heard in opera. The king of the Feared dropped to his knees, yowling in pain and defeat, sending his angry wind whipping toward the group. Emmy and Archie dropped, but Jainey held her voice steady.

Joe burst, becoming nothing more than dust.

Jainey slumped, wobbling from exerting so much power. Her little sister ran to catch her. She eased her to the ground, and they looked around at the fallen fae, each one processing the events.

"What was that?" Emmeline asked her sister.

The older girl, still exhausted, smiled weakly. "Mrs. Bartlet had been trying to recruit me, not for the choir, but to coach me in chanting."

"Chanting?" Archie asked.

"A form of singing infused with magic."

"Y … you have magic?" Emmeline knelt beside her.

Jainey nodded, panting with exhaustion. "I was reluctant to believe at first, but I began having dreams, just like you."

"You were from our time?" Emmeline swallowed hard. "Why didn't you say anything? You made me believe you thought I was crazy."

"I was still in denial, I guess. After hearing it from you guys," she nodded to Archie and George, "confirmed my dreams were memories. I called Mrs. Bartlet right after and told her I want to take the lessons. Turns out I'm a fast learner."

"And you worked at the bank to watch over her, huh?" Emmeline looked at the wizard, who smiled. "I don't remember you." Emmy shook her head at Jainey. "I don't have memories of you."

"Think hard, My Lady," Jainey said, mimicking her Scottish accent.

"My … no way. *You* were my lady in waiting."

Emmeline blinked, shocked, then snickered.

"Laugh now, but when we get back, don't expect me to carry your fancy dresses, got it, loser?"

Em threw her arms around Jainey, who embraced her back.

"Geoffrey." Emmeline pulled away. "What was the prophecy Joe spoke of?"

"A child will be born - one who will change the course of time and fate." The wizard's wounds had healed much quicker than any mere mortal, though his torn clothes still showed deep cuts.

"He told me he wanted my child, but I didn't know what he meant."

"The baby will be a threat to the dark fae's existence - to evil, itself. They will be powerless against the child as it grows."

"Will the baby have magic?"

"So the prophecy says." Geoffrey pulled a pocket watch out and jumped up. "We need to go, *now*."

"The moon, hurry now, children." Grandfather hustled to the door, not a limp or hobble.

"Your leg," Archie gazed at George's perfectly healthy leg, then looked at the sword lying on the ground and picked it up.

"Allistair sent you with as much protection as he could," the wizard said, ushering them out the door.

- ༄༅ ༄ ༄ -

"Bartlet will be waiting for us." Geoffrey said after they

piled into the car and started off.

"Where?"

"The beach. We have a window of an hour after the blood moon appears."

Emmeline turned and kissed Archie with a burst of excitement.

"Remember, I'm not your servant when we get home, got it?" Jainey poked the girl in the arm.

"Got it. You can be my sister."

Jainey smiled and looked to the front as the car rushed down a deserted road. They screeched to a halt and Geoffrey announced, "Here we are."

The group ran through the deep, cold sand toward Mrs. Bartlet holding a glowing stone.

"At last," she said. "I'm sorry I couldn't be with you at the cellar, but I had every confidence in you, and, well, you did it!" She brought Jainey in for a hug. Then she addressed the rest of the group. "The blood moon will show at any moment. We must be ready."

"Are you from our time, Mrs. Bartlet?" Emmeline asked.

"No, but we're family, a few times removed. One of the Caliburns married a Bartlet. Jainey, here, is a Bartlet."

"Hold up, that means we're family, so why the hell was I a servant?" Jainey placed a hand on her hip.

"Your parents passed away when you were very young. Allistair, your second cousin, took you in, though he couldn't raise you as a daughter, for the same reason he couldn't claim his own daughter. He wanted to protect you both from the consequences of magic."

"Cool, so I washed Em's undergarments and said, 'yes miss' and 'no miss' all because my cousin didn't want me to know I had powers?"

"Dramatic much?" Emmeline gave her a small push. "If my memory serves right, you were given the same lush treatment as me. And I'm pretty sure ladies in waiting don't do laundry."

"Yeah, yeah," Jainey teased and waved her hand lazily.

"All right," Emmeline turned back to Mrs. Bartlet. "Jainey and I are cousins, correct?"

"That's right. The Bartlets held the gift of chanting, while the Caliburns had the gift of enchanting."

"Quite the bloodline you have there." George chortled. "Sorry, Archibald, the Emsworths hold no special gifts such as that."

"What are you talking about? Clearly we hold the good looks." Archie winked playfully at Emmeline.

A sharp light caught their attention.

"Be ready," Mrs. Bartlet warned as she held up the stone, igniting in the greatest orange-red color Emmeline had ever seen. She took Jainey's hand as Archie locked his fingers in her other. A tornado-like wave formed in the ocean, and the woman threw the stone into it, causing a swirling light to emerge, making an arch that spanned at least fifteen feet across the water.

Geoffrey looked back. "It was a pleasure meeting you all. I'll not let your story be forgotten. Now go, live your lives."

Hand in hand, the four walked toward the portal. They stopped when a shrill sound, *that* sound - the wailing of a demon - enclaved the beach. It jolted Emmeline's heart, sending the familiar snake of dread slithering down her spine. She looked up to see five enormous, winged creatures.

"Get back," the wizard screamed as he shot a bolt above them. Archie pulled his wife behind him and lifted the silver sword.

"Joe ambushed us. He knew he might not have a chance, so he held the strongest back as a last resort to keep us from going home," Geoffrey concluded, again zapping at the beasts.

A fae lunged at Archie, grabbing his arm. The sword fell into the shallow water, and Emmeline grabbed it up, her arms feeling like jello from wielding the heavy weapon earlier, and swung. The fae cackled but moved back enough for her to pull Archie away.

"Thanks," he said, out of breath.

"Jainey, sing," Mrs. Bartlet demanded.

Together, they began chanting. The Feared covered their ears, screeching in pain. One fae circled Emmeline and Archie while another beat his giant wings, creating waves, making Jainey falter in her song. Mrs. Bartlet looked at Geoffrey with an expression Emmeline couldn't decide was fear, defeat, hopelessness, or all three.

"Take your sword," Geoffrey told the boy.

Archie took it and fought alongside the wizard, keeping two of the black beasts away from Emmeline and George, while Jainey and Bartlet fought the others with their melody. The woman looked at Geoffrey again and made a nodding motion at George.

"George, go, go now," Geoffrey called to the old man, firing bolts of lightning at the monsters fluttering before them.

"Not without my grandson!"

"We need him here to …" Geoffrey was struck down. "No, stay where you are," he coughed out when Archie turned to help him. Mrs. Bartlet and Jainey were getting winded as their battle song rang out, holding the dark demons off as long as they could.

"Grandfather, I have to be the last to go." Archie's eyes drooped, as if those words were the last he'd ever choose to say. "This sword has powers incomparable to other weapons." Archie's hair, like everyone else's, whipped around as the portal swirled, and as the ocean rolled, and as the Feared sacrificed themselves to their cause.

"Not without my boy," Grandfather repeated, but the wizard leaped forward and pushed him into the blue abyss.

"Girls, now," he yelled to Emmeline and Jainey, then, with full force, unleashed his fury on the dark fae. Mrs. Bartlet took Jainey's hand and led her to the portal, giving her a quick hug and a kiss.

Jainey wrapped her hand around Emmeline's wrist and tugged her, but Em planted her feet in the shifting sand, shaking her head, causing her tears to weave zigzag down her cheeks.

"You have to go," Archie screamed to Emmeline as the fae dodged his swings.

"I'm not leaving you."

"Please, please," he begged, eyeing a weakening Bartlet and Geoffrey. "The portal won't close for another half hour." Archie's raised voice was just barely audible over the yells, crashing waves, and chanting. "We have to prevent them from following us, and they," he nodded toward Mrs. Bartlet and the wizard, "can't do it by themselves."

"I can help, I can call the bees, or wolves, or the damn sharks ..."

"I'll follow you, but for now, I have to stay. Please," he implored her again, his feet slipping in the thick, wet sand.

Geoffrey created a rope-like light and thrashed it above Archie's head, pulling a fae away before it could attack. The wizard slammed the creature to the ground, destroying it. Archie ran to Emmeline, leaned down, and kissed her like they were the only two standing on the beach. When he pulled away, he looked at Jainey and nodded.

She grabbed Em's hand and dove into the portal, pulling a screaming Emmy with her.

"Don't forget me," Archie's voice echoed through the tunnel, then faded as pink and purple and blue surrounded her.

Clouds – soft, wispy clouds shrouded her - the mist kissed her cheeks, wiping away the blood and dirt. She floated, weightless, as if she were laying in a lazy river. Then visions appeared. She saw herself as a little girl, standing next to Allistair as he gently placed a bumblebee in her hand.

"Cute little Fuzzy Buzzy," Emmeline's small voice said.

The next one was Allistair twirling her in the drawing-room while Joe sat, filling himself with wine and food. Then came a vision of a teenage Emmeline peeking through the keyhole to the drawing room as Joseph and Allistair argued. She remembered that moment, though then she couldn't make out what they were saying. Now, as she watched the scene play out like a movie, she heard it all.

"I told you to stop, Joseph. You promised, you promised." Allistair was distraught.

Joe only smirked.

"My own brother … I defended you. I protected you."

"Oh, come now, Allistair. You're upset because I am now as powerful as you."

"Giving yourself to the occult, to those *creatures*, is not what I'd call powerful. It wasn't my choice to be born with the gift, but I embraced it."

"And I embrace mine!" Joe boomed.

"It is not in good nature, brother! Please, try to see reason. No amount of magic is worth giving up your soul."

"Oh, dear brother, that's where you're wrong." Joe gave a deep, horrendous chuckle, and left. For good.

Emmeline continued through the portal clouds, a realm made of time and memories. The visions with Allistair made her realize that he'd always treated her as a daughter. Joe had never raised her, nor did he ever care for her. She became lost in the scenes of her life, not knowing if she was a ghost roaming through space or if she was a real, solid person.

"Raise her as your own." Allistair, cheeks wet with tears, placed a swaddled infant in a young Joseph's arms.

"She must never know," the great wizard whispered to his brother.

"Has she exhibited powers already?" Joseph marveled

at baby Emmeline.

"Only five months old and the birds treat her as a queen. Yes, she is strong."

"Magnificent," the younger brother breathed, staring at the child as if she were a prize.

"I implore you not to let on. You know the ramifications of magical people in our world. They will use her or shun her. She will become a target."

"My mouth is sealed."

Sailing through the clouds brought Emmeline the realization that this portal was catered to her and her questions. They were not only her memories but the answers to everything she wanted to know, and things she *needed* to know.

"Do we really need all these servants?" Emmeline asked Archie as she surveyed the assembly of people whisking through the substantial manor doors. They were in the midst of moving in, just days before their wedding.

Emmeline, still drifting down the stream of memories, watched her past self below.

Servants carried elegant chairs and paintings into the manor. Maids dashed around with fresh sheets and new taper candles to replace the old. Windows were being scrubbed, baskets of vegetables and hooks of meat were taken to the kitchens.

"This seems like too much. We only need a few, really." She wrinkled her nose, feeling uncomfortable and a bit pretentious for having far more than they need.

"Sweetheart," Archie said, peering around, then gently took her shoulder and accompanied her to an empty room. "Of course, we don't need so much, but we have the means to give work … *good* pay. If I can spare any coin to give people quality of life, I'm going to."

Emmeline loosened her hardened expression and brushed his cheek. "A nobleman like no other." She touched her lips to his, and the memory grew dim and vanished.

Another vision floated forward. Emmeline laid on a soft mattress with silk bed curtains around her, blowing in a cool, spring breeze. A smile of familiarity pulled at her lips.

"Emmeline!" a voice bellowed. The person jumped on the bed and wrapped their arms around her.

"Jainey?" Emmeline grumbled as she sat up. "What …" her breath caught when she saw candles, fabric chairs, and ornate rugs covering an old, wooden floor. This was no vision. She looked at Jainey. The older girl was dressed in a blue gown, her hair hanging over her shoulder in a long braid.

"We made it home." Em blinked rapidly, like she was trying to wake from a long sleep.

"I thought you were dead."

Emmy tilted her head.

"It's been five months since I arrived home. You were with me, and then you weren't. Allistair and Grandfather George have been beside themselves, what with you and Archie disappearing completely."

Emmeline clenched her jaw, her breath quickening.

"I've been in that portal for months? Wait … Archie isn't here?"

Jainey shook her head.

"He's probably still in there somewhere. Maybe it'll take him longer since he was the last to leave." Emmeline gulped but forced her sentence out with hopefulness.

"Come on. Father and Grandfather George will be thrilled you're here."

Emmeline raised her brow at the girl.

"Hey, you said I could be your sister when we came back. Allistair felt the same. So yeah, I call him father." She grinned. "Up you go." Jainey held out a hand to help the girl up. "Oh, my God!" She choked when Emmeline stood from the bed.

Emmeline looked down to see her stomach had grown. "I'm …" She shot her gaze at Jainey. "I'm pregnant."

Chapter 18

Days or weeks had gone by, Emmeline's frantic mind couldn't keep track. Every sunrise had her searching her father's manor to see if Archie had made it home, but he was nowhere to be found. She would visit the manor that was to be her home after the wedding, but only furniture covered with cloth remained in the quiet home.

"Emmeline," Allistair addressed her at dinner one evening. "Let's take a walk. Show me your deer."

Emmeline took her father to a clearing on the property where she'd been playing with the wildlife when she needed a break from her worries. A herd of white-tailed deer crunched through the forest leaves and greeted them.

Allistair, delighted, rubbed their necks. "You always have amazed me, daughter." He turned to the girl, who was being nudged by a fawn. "I am ferociously proud of you. I hope you can one day forgive me."

She knew he meant not claiming her as his own and hiding these magnificent powers from her.

She placed her hand over his. "There's nothing to forgive. Though I didn't know you were my father, you still treated me like your child. Joe never did."

Allistair wrapped his burly arms around Emmeline and kissed her head. "Had I known who my brother truly was, I would have done things differently."

"Did you know about this prophecy?" She pulled away and rubbed her pregnant belly.

"I learned of it the night of your wedding."

Emmeline situated herself on a rock and brushed the fur on a deer who laid its head in her lap.

"You and Archibald had left the wedding banquet and were on your way to Isle of Mull for your honeymoon. Our guests had departed, but one visitor stayed behind. He revealed his disguise. My brother, Joseph."

Emmeline gulped.

"He informed me that a witch with the gift of future sight warned them of their demise in the form of a wizard - one who was greater than all who ever lived. The Foreseer declared a child would be born. The grandchild of the Great Wizard, she told my brother."

"Which pointed him to your only child: me."

Allistair sat on a fallen tree and bowed his head. "My name should have been the Great Fool. I beseeched Joseph to come back to the family. I hadn't known that my brother had been long gone before he even became a man. I would not give him your whereabouts, though he threatened my life. We were interrupted by one of his fae followers. They'd found you."

"How?"

"Sir Angus Bayne."

The name brought the man's face to her mind. "Father, Sir Angus attacked Archie in the forest as we were riding."

"He also released a prisoner to act as your mother."

"Maud, oh my God. I watched the news, why didn't I recognize her at first?"

"Joseph was particularly good at altering reality."

"Did she know?"

"She did not. Her mind was spellbound."

"She said some weird things to Jainey and me one day. Then Joe found a convenient little wine stand."

"Found, or created?" Allistair leaned forward.

She slightly bobbed her head in agreement.

"Joseph left directly after Angus had betrayed us. I followed them, though their wings helped them escape. When I found you, they were feeding on your souls."

Emmeline held her neck and grimaced.

"I fought them off long enough to send you through a portal under the blood moon, but the fae slipped through at the last minute. I immediately sent out trackers to locate my cousins, Isla, who married a Bartlet, and Ronan, who produced the line Geoffrey was born into. They graciously agreed to teach their young children of the prophecy, and to share the stories of Archibald and Emmeline Emsworth. For centuries, the Bartlets and Caliburns handed down the stories, teachings, and conferment of powers, though with each generation the magic transferred to only a few people. The ones who knew the truth prepared for the arrival of you two and practiced to become protectors."

"A thousand years. Wow. They certainly came through for us." Emmeline thought for a moment as the deer grazed beside her. "Why did you send Jainey and Grandfather?"

"I didn't want you two to be alone out there. I was unsure if you'd know who you are, or if you had new memories." He took in a breath. "I thought sending you far into the future, as far as my powers would let me, would keep you safe. My dear daughter, I am sorry I couldn't protect you from those monsters who invaded your home."

Emmeline knelt in front of him and took his hands. "You *did* protect us. How you managed to keep the story of us alive *and* believable until it reached Mrs. Bartlet and Geoffrey amazes me! And Grandfather George's cane, absolutely genius."

Allistair confirmed George's limp had been only to hide the weapon. "It had to be disguised. One would question a man walking around with a sword, would they not?"

Em grinned and laid her head on her father's shoulder, pulling a carrot from her bag to feed the deer.

Chapter 19

Summer had come and Emmeline was inching closer to giving birth, but she ignored it most days. Instead, she spent her time in the library, attempting to find *anything* on time travel and portals. Her father tried to reason with her that opening a portal took practice, many, many years of practice.

"I'm sorry, daughter, but I no longer have the powers I once did," he told her.

Emmeline grew frustrated and told herself there must be a way to get Archie back. She refused to give up hope.

A hand rapped on the door one evening as she paced her room.

"Come in." Emmeline tied her robe around her stomach which looked more like a hot air balloon at this point.

"Hello, my dear." Grandfather walked in and took a seat in a cushioned chair, patting the one next to him.

"My dear Emmeline," he began, placing his wrinkled hand over hers after she'd lowered herself into the chair. "Your baby will be here soon."

She looked down. "I know," she said, her words hushed.

"We must move on, my child."

"No, I …" Her words stuck in her throat, and her skin turned cold.

He squeezed her hand lovingly. "We will never forget him, and I know he will be with us forever." He pointed at her belly. "This baby that you are carrying is a piece of him – a piece that you can kiss and love and cherish. You will see Archibald in this babe's face."

A lump formed in her throat.

"He wouldn't wish this sadness upon you."

"I don't want to give up hope."

"I'm not saying to forget about him, but right now you need to focus on your child."

She knew he was right. She'd driven herself nearly mad with all the research. She ignored the cramps and back pain. She didn't even give notice to the large mound which prevented her from turning comfortably in bed.

After Grandfather left, she placed a hand over the bump. Something moved.

"Oh my God," she gasped. Jainey had just opened the door and dashed to her side.

"What is it? Are you okay?"

"I felt it. I felt the baby kick."

Jainey's face lit up like an evening star as Emmeline took her hand and placed it over the spot. "I felt it, too," she shrieked with mirth.

Emmeline felt a spark of joy. She'd finally allowed herself to accept the truth.

"Jainey, I'm having a baby," she said out loud.

"I know, Fool."

"No, I'm *having* a baby, like right now," she yelped the last word in pain. Jainey ran from the room.

The pain progressed rapidly until the breath was

knocked out of her. She fell to the floor, gasping through unimaginable agony. Her vision blurred as people lifted her to the bed and pressed a cold cloth to her forehead.

"Emmeline," a voice said, sounding far from her. It called for her again. She opened her eyes to see green fields. The voice said her name a third time. Archie walked toward her within a glowing light. He knelt beside her.

"You're here." Her voice was weak as she cried. "I should," she struggled to sit up, "beat you with a wet rag for making me worry."

"Don't forget me."

"How can I when I'm staring at you?"

"Don't forget me," he repeated, and vanished. She found herself in her room, a nursemaid was changing blankets beneath her.

She squeezed her eyes shut and opened them.

Jainey walked to her, holding a bundled blanket. "It's a boy," she said, leaning down to hand Emmeline a newborn. The new mother took the baby and began weeping. She kissed his soft, fuzzy head and held him close, now knowing she could love once again.

Chapter 20

"My turn," Jainey said, walking into Emmeline's room. "Grandfather needs his herbs. I thought you could use some fresh air. Father and I will take the baby to meet the bees."

"The bees, Jainey? He's only three months old."

"Well, he's already able to sing like me. Just yesterday he was cooing, and the window flew open bringing in some serious wind."

Emmeline laughed. "Last week I was blowing raspberries, and he got so excited, kicking his legs, that all the candles in the room lit up."

"This nugget inherited *all* the family powers. So, he probably has your affinity for animals."

"True." Emmeline kissed her son and handed him to Jainey. "But if anything starts to go wrong, you get him out of there. I don't want him stung."

"I'll sing the buzzies to sleep." Jainey winked and bounced the baby in her arms as she left the room. Emmeline wrapped a shawl around her shoulders and walked down the stairs.

"Ready to go?" she asked George. He held out his arm, and they strolled into town.

"Look," she gasped, pointing at a shop window. "I'll be right back."

"Well now, isn't that wonderful," he commented as she came out, holding a bee-carved rattle. "The babe will love it."

They continued through the village when Grandfather halted and wobbled. He touched a shaky hand to his lips, and he cried out.

"Grandfather, are you alright?" Emmeline took his elbow to steady him but noticed the pale shock in his eyes. She turned to see what he was looking at. A young man stood in the middle of the market square, his clothes filthy. He seemed to be selling vegetables to a vendor.

Emmeline inched forward in disbelief. She stood a few feet behind him, not able to move any further. Her joints and face were like stone. She could barely breathe. He turned and she swallowed.

He tilted his head slightly as he took in her features, like he had met her once. Then he politely smiled and walked past her.

"Archie," she forced herself to say through a dry throat.

He turned, furrowing his brow. "Have we met?"

Again, she swallowed. Archie looked at the wooden toy in her hands.

"What's that?"

"A rattle." Emmeline's mind couldn't find the words to make him remember. "It's a rattle," she repeated.

"A bee."

"Uh, yes." She ran her fingers over the hollowed marks in the wood.

"A bee …" His eyes darted around the ground, then he shot his head up, locking eyes with hers. "Fuzzy buzzy?"

Emmeline nearly dropped the toy and nodded, tears filling her eyes.

"Eh … Emmy? Yes, Emmy!" His face glowed as every memory danced in his crystal eyes, brightened as his memories returned.

Emmeline jumped into his arms, brushing her lips against his. He enveloped her in a tight hug and returned her kiss. Grandfather wrapped his arms around them, much like when Archie had forgotten her the first time, but this time George was laughing, crying, and rejoicing.

"How did you make it? We thought you were dead." Emmeline kissed him again.

"We defeated them. They're gone." He stood back and looked at her. "I saw you. We were losing, but I saw you standing in the fog with someone. A man."

"Allistair?"

Archie shook his head. "He looked like me, almost. He had my eyes. The Feared saw him, too. They seemed terrified and angrier than ever. I remember one of them blasting me down. The man next to you, he did something after I fell - said something, yelled something …" Archie shook his head. "Whatever it was, it burst every one of the Feared into ashes. Geoffrey screamed at me to go. I barely made it to the portal. After that, I was here - a farmer."

"That blast must have taken your memory. Their last attempt to keep you two apart," Grandfather said. "Their last attempt to keep the prophecy from happening." George smirked at Emmeline who still clutched the rattle.

She took Archie's hand. "Arch, the prophecy is true. I … we have a baby."

111

Archie's knees gave out, but Grandfather caught him.

"How?" His eyes bulged. "We've been gone for months, or centuries. I'm confused."

"Our, uh, honeymoon, I'm guessing. It makes sense now why Sir Angus followed us into the woods the next day. They'd been watching us."

Archie took a deep breath and looked at her stomach, then to her joy-filled face. "You, uh … you're not …"

"I had him over three months ago."

"A boy," he stated, a smile pulling at his lips.

"Come on." She grabbed his hand and yanked him along.

- ᎤᏍᏂᏬᏋ -

"Welcome back, my son." Allistair embraced Archie as they entered the manor. "Happiness cannot begin to describe my emotions."

"Is Jainey upstairs?" Emmeline asked.

"Yes. Go meet your child," Allistair patted Archie on the back, then stood with George and watched the couple ascend the staircase.

Jainey screamed with bliss when he came through the door and jumped into his arms. He squeezed her tight, but his eyes were on the cradle. She moved to the side so Archie could meet his child. He peeked in at the crystal-eyed baby.

"Wanna hold him?" Emmeline whispered, admiring the proud smile on her husband's face.

Archie reached in, lifting him into his arms. He let the

baby clutch his finger. "He's strong."

"In more ways than one," Jainey commented.

Emmeline wrapped her arm around Archie's back and looked down at their son, whose eyes went from his mother to his father. He wiggled, then cooed and smiled. The baby squealed like he was laughing.

"Whoa," Jainey said as the candles ignited, shining brighter than the sun. A sweet-smelling breeze entered the room, wrapping around the family. Birds landed on the window, singing and fluttering their wings while a swarm of bees looped around the room. Wolves howled in unison, a celebratory sound. Stars shot across the midday sky.

As the baby continued his joyous noises, Emmeline heard faint conversations. Archie must have heard it too because he looked around the room, which was now filled with voices, Emmeline and Archie's - Allistair's and Jainey's and Grandfather's. Em focused. She realized they were memories playing out. The happiest times of her life. The little baby Archie held was conjuring every form of love Emmeline had ever known.

Archie beamed at his wife. "What do you call him?"

She ran her fingers over the baby's cheek, then brushed his head with her hand. "Merlin."

ABOUT THE AUTHOR

V. Mull, born in 1991, began writing at the young age of five. She often finds inspiration for her many stories within the beautiful woods of Maine where she lives with her husband, three children, and pets.

Mull pens a few different genres such as Young Adult Fantasy, New Adult Fantasy, and Childrens' Stories. In 2019 her short story titled "The Queen and the Pebble" won first place in Pixie Forest Publishing's Summer contest, and her short story, Don't Turn Around, was published in Pixie Forest Publishing's anthology, Phobia! An Anthology of Fear.

Mull's greatest wish is to create a world into which people can escape, and she will continue to work hard to make that dream come true.

Liked this book?
Please leave a review!

Reviews are important to authors and publishers.
Please take a moment to leave a review on Amazon and/or Goodreads.

They help authors sell more books.

20-25 reviews and Amazon includes the book in the "Also Bought" and
"You Might Like" lists.
50-70 reviews and Amazon highlights the book in spotlight positions
and in its newsletter.

Thank you!